A. Edmiston

THREE STORIES OF ROMANCE

THREE STORIES OF ROMANCE

By

WARWICK DEEPING
GILBERT FRANKAU
AND
ETHEL MANNIN

DAILY EXPRESS FICTION LIBRARY

Printed in Great Britain

FOREWORD

THE three love stories included in this volume are each of them excellent examples of the work of the respective authors under whose names they appear.

There is probably no severer test of the ability of a novel-writer than the short story. In order to succeed in this form of fiction, it is necessary to arrest the immediate attention of the reader. The story must be concise and yet complete. In short, to achieve a satisfactory result the writer must be a master of his art. Those who have excelled in this particular branch of story-telling are to be found among the greatest literary figures of their day. Names that immediately spring to the mind include Rudyard Kipling with his "Soldiers Three," "Plain Tales from the Hills," etc. Sir James Barrie with his "Auld Licht Idylls" and his One Act Plays, which stand in the same position to the Three Act Play as the short story does to the full length novel.

In America there is Brett Hart and O. Henry. In France, Alphonse Daudet and Anatole France. And in Germany, Arthur Schnitzler. All are famous novelists in their respective countries.

The following three love stories are set on the sunny shores of the blue Mediterranean. The martyrdom of Elsie Parsloe, the young wife of the elderly and morose Dr. Jacob Parsloe, takes place in a "castle" beyond Genoa where the Professor isolates his young bride. Their Villa Pineta, with its romantic half-wild garden, its pines, ilexes, cypresses and its classic temple half hidden by arbutus and box, overlooks another villa on the opposite cliff and "thereby hangs a tale."

The Judas Tree, which at the time of this happening was just in bloom, sheltered a mysterious house that stood high above the Route Nationale amid vineyards and grey-green olives, with a triangle of blue Mediterranean pinched between red cliff fangs. It is here the owner unburdens himself of his extraordinary love story.

And it is in the picturesque little Italian seaside town of Rapallo that Ishbel Hedley hears the strains of Forbidden Music.

Mr. Warwick Deeping, who was born in 1877, began life as a doctor. After taking his degree at Cambridge he studied medicine at the Middlesex Hospital and afterwards practised as a doctor for a year or more. As you will notice, his chief character in "Martyrdom" is a doctor—Dr. Parslowe. For about twenty-five years or so his novels have been extremely popular. His best-known story, "Sorrell and Son," is one of his many "best sellers."

Mr. Gilbert Frankau also took to novel writing on second thoughts, as so many of our famous novelists have done. He was born in 1884 and inherited the gift of writing from his mother, who was the well-known novelist, Frank Danby.

Both Mr. Warwick Deeping and Mr. Gilbert Frankau served in the War and both of them managed to continue their output in spite of the fact.

Miss Ethel Mannin, whose books have a tremendous hold on the public, is undoubtedly one of the most famous women writers of the day. Her first story was written at the age of ten, appearing on the Children's Page in the *Lady's Companion*. Since then her output has been steady and her success has grown greater each year. Her motto, as she says, is "Work all day and every day and type everything straight from brain to typewriter."

THE EDITOR.

MARTYRDOM

By WARWICK DEEPING

MARTYRDOM

CHAPTER I

Dr. Jacob Parsloe stepped off the bus where Putney High Street joins Richmond Road. It was raining and Dr. Parsloe put up his umbrella. He had the air of a man who is displeased with his surroundings, especially with Putney and the rain.

Sighting a policeman on the other side of the road, he crossed it, frowning resentfully at the traffic, for a philosopher may be a most unphilosophic person where crude, material happenings jostle him.

"Can you direct me to Rufus Road?"

The constable gave him the necessary information as though he were reading from a guide book.

"How far is it?"

"About a mile."

Dr. Parsloe grunted and took the middle of the pavement. He was a big man, clumsily built, and he wore his black clothes clumsily, almost as though he slept in them. They bagged at the knees, and bulged at the elbows. He walked fast, with his head forward and his umbrella held like a shield. He ignored the other people on the pavement, and ignored them so thoroughly that, menaced by the masked and advancing bulk of him, they gave way. It had taken Dr. Parsloe three years to write that epoch-making book of his, "The Variations of Vitalism." He was a truculent thinker, and he walked as he thought, ignoring irrelevant trivialities.

His big white face looked more fiercely serious than usual, and fifteen years of such seriousness had made him appear ten years older than he was, for Parsloe was just fifty. He had a tonsure, and the figure and hands of a man who had never played games.

"Confound it," he reflected, "I suppose I shall have to do something! After all I did promise Lorrimer I would do something. One ought to be more cautious in making promises."

Turning a corner he charged into somebody else's umbrella, and it was the other man who lost his hat.

"You ought to keep to the left, sir. Why don't you look where you are going?"

Parsloe did not apologize; he never apologized to anyone.

"I always keep in the middle of the path. I think you must have been doing the same thing."

"Look at my hat!" snapped the injured one, fishing it out of the gutter.

Parsloe gave it a glance of disdain.

"I suggest that you dry it before you try to brush it," he observed, and left the other man standing.

He resumed the reflections which had been interrupted by this incident, reflections upon the responsibility which was being thrust upon him by a promise given in his more generous and expansive youth. He had never expected John Lorrimer to die, and still less had he expected that his widow would follow him at the end of five years, leaving a child behind her. The facts were that Catharine Lorrimer was dying: that she appeared to have no relations; that the child was unprovided for; that she had appealed to her husband's friend. Parsloe was a man of means. His father, a boot manufacturer, had left him fifteen hundred a year.

"It's a scandal," he thought, "these improvident marriages!"

His face darkened. Years ago he had thought of marrying, and had become engaged to be married to a woman who had finally confessed with almost hysterical passion that he was not the sort of man whom a woman could marry. The insult had rankled. He had despised women ever since, and yet the incident had left in him a grievance against women, a sore spot in his ego-complex. There were times when he wished to possess a woman, to dominate her, enslave her, make her pay for the secretly-nursed insult the whole sex had flung at him in the person of one woman. He had the makings of a tyrant. Even his thinking was tyrannical and profoundly arrogant.

Five minutes later he found himself outside No. 17 Rufus Road, a red and yellow villa in a row of red and yellow villas, each with a doormat of a garden spread under a cramped bow window. Jacob Parsloe rang the bell and closed his umbrella, and when a tired-eyed servant opened the door to him he thrust his hat and umbrella upon her as though she were no more than a hat-stand.

"Mrs. Lorrimer expects me. I am Dr Parsloe."

He was not an observant man, but when he was taken into that upper room where Catharine Lorrimer lay dying he was aware of her as a pair of eyes—eyes of waiting and suspense. She was the mere shadow of a woman, and the colour of parchment, and all that was left of her seemed to dwell in her eyes.

"It's such a relief—your coming. I'm so grateful."

Her voice was a little husky whisper. She was afraid of him, and yet she compelled herself to seem unafraid, for he was the one person on the earth who had the power to conjure away another and a far greater fear. She looked at him with her beseeching eyes.

Jacob Parsloe sat down. There were a score of things which he might have observed and did not observe, things which would have touched the ordinary plain man who did not sit enthroned on a transcendental egotism.

"This is deplorable," he said, "very deplorable. How long have you been ill?"

"About a year."

"H'm, about a year. Dear me."

He sat and stared at her as though the soul of her was a closed book which he did not care to read.

"Am I to understand that the child——?"

Her eyelids flickered.

"It was about Elsie. I would never have troubled you but for her. She will be stranded—utterly stranded."

"Dear me. You have not saved anything?"

"I couldn't, not from my small annuity. If only——"

Her voice died away. She lay and watched him with a kind of voiceless anguish, feeling the hardness of the man yet trying to believe that he was not hard.

"Elsie. So that is her name. I had almost forgotten."

"You are her god-father."

He ignored the reminder, and sat with folded hands, frowning.

"Let me see, how old is she?"

"Twelve."

"Twelve! As old as that!"

He appeared to reflect.

"Supposing I see her."

The woman in the bed made a sudden movement as though she had been waiting for some heartening ray of sunlight and seized the suggestive hope of it when it came. She knocked feebly on the wall at the head of her bed.

"She—she's such a gentle child," she said.

A girl came into the room, a girl with a mass of chestnut hair, dark eyes and a pale face. She was frightened; she had been crying herself to sleep at nights, and she looked like a little fragile ghost. Dr. Parsloe and this child examined each other. He looked very large and solemn to Elsie Lorrimer, and his great white face with its bald forehead and jug-shaped chin—it had the appearance of a bag hanging below his mouth—was vaguely terrifying. His large nose seemed to reach out at her; his grey eyes made her think of the ground-glass panels in the bath-room window.

"So this is Elsie."

He held out a hand, and her half-shrinking fingers were momentarily engulfed in it.

"How do you do, Elsie?"

And suddenly, she burst into tears, and hid her face on her mother's pillow.

"Dear, dear!" said Parsloe, "a little overwrought—I presume."

Kate Lorrimer laid a thin hand on the child's head.

"There—there, you mustn't cry; you must be a brave girl. Mr. Parsloe is a friend of your daddy's. It was very kind of him to come."

Parsloe sat and watched them, and his glassy eyes took note of the young girl with a sudden human attentiveness. Something had happened to him. An idea had exploded inside the profound emptiness of him, a very extraordinary and suggestive idea. He sat and smiled. He contemplated the lapse of time, eight years, a girl with lengthened skirts and burgeoning bosom; a meek girl, gentle, docile, properly disciplined, a pleasant hand-maid, a slave. And why should it not be so? The girl's fragile richness, her delicate colouring, her tears, her abandonment, piqued him.

It would be pleasant to possess something so completely that he would feel revenged upon the whole despicable sex.

"I'm afraid I have frightened her," he said.

"Oh, no; it is only that—— Elsie, dear."

The child sat up with a sudden rigid courage.

"Elsie, dear, come and kiss your godfather."

She looked at Parsloe; her eyes seemed blind; and then—obediently—she came and kissed his bald forehead.

"That's right," and he patted her shoulder. "Run away, dear; I want to talk to your mother."

She went, and Parsloe, turning to the bed with a sort of pleasant unctiousness, gave the dying woman the promise that she yearned for.

"I will look after the child. I will have her educated."

Catharine Lorrimer's eyes lost their stare of suspense.

"God bless you," she said; "you don't know what a weight you have taken off my heart."

CHAPTER II

THREE days later Catharine Lorrimer died, and a very bewildered and miserable child was taken by Jacob Parsloe to an hotel in Bloomsbury. In the taxi she clutched a little wet ball of a handkerchief, and lay back in her corner like a bird crouching in the corner of a cage. Parsloe tried to be fatherly, though Elsie's grief embarrassed him, and even when granting the naturalness of her grief he decided that a girl should be taught to control her emotions.

"My dear," he said, "try to be a brave little girl."

She did not want to be brave; she wanted to be comforted.

"Miss Nimfrey is waiting to take care of you. She is very kind. Be a brave girl."

At the Burton Hotel Elsie had her first meeting with Norah Nimfrey. She was a cousin of Jacob Parsloe's, and partly dependent upon the great man who had summoned her from Waddington, in Sussex, and installed her for a week in a little private suite at the Burton. It was here that she fell upon Elsie and enveloped her, mingling her straw-grey hair with the child's bronze curls, and showing to Elsie a pair of short-sighted blue eyes magnified by rimless pince-nez.

"My poor dear child!"

Miss Nimfrey was a mixture of sentimentality and hardness, but Elsie was too desperately in need of sympathy to be aware of the hardness. She surrendered to Miss Nimfrey; she accepted her—high forehead, pince-nez, lipless mouth and all—and clung to her from that moment. She was gentle and impressionable, a virgin book. What Miss Nimfrey chose to write in her was written and became the law of the great man who wrote other sorts of books.

For Jacob Parsloe had a lengthy talk with his cousin on the evening after Catharine Lorrimer's funeral. Elsie was to find a home with Norah Nimfrey in the cottage at Waddington, and to be educated there by Miss Nimfrey in person.

and Parsloe promised to allow her another one hundred and fifty pounds a year.

"I want her to be educated as a woman should be educated. She must be docile and sweet tempered. She must know how to obey and to serve."

Miss Nimfrey wrinkled up her high forehead.

"You don't wish her to be modern?"

"She must be brought up in the convent idea. No mixing with boys, or with other girls unless those girls are most carefully selected. Let her learn Italian and French and a little music, and how to cook and look after a house. But—docility—obedience."

His cousin felt that there was something at the back of the great man's mind, and having a high admiration for him and being partly dependent on his bounty, she wished to be in a position to satisfy his ideals.

"Would you mind telling me, Jacob, what kind of future you contemplate for the child? If I have your end in view——"

"I contemplate marrying her. I am paying you the compliment of asking you to educate my future wife."

Miss Nimfrey was not a little taken aback, but it was no business of hers to appear astonished at the very original attitude of a great man. After all, what could be sounder than the proper education of a partner who was to take her place in so serious an alliance?

"The responsibility is a heavy one, Jacob. I wish to be clear upon one point. Is Elsie to know? What I mean is——"

"Certainly she must know. I wish that to be the central idea of her life. Everything else must be built round it. But keep her—innocent—quite unspotted. You understand?"

"Yes," said Miss Nimfrey; "I think I understand."

So Elsie was spirited away to Miss Nimfrey's prim little cottage on the outskirts of Waddington, and Dr. Parsloe paid them a visit before returning to Italy and his thinker's castle by the sea. He spent nine months of the year in Italy and three in England, declaring with great seriousness that he could think only in the sun. He took several country walks with Elsie, showing himself heavily and paternally playful, and when he left her gave her a kiss, a sovereign, and some significant advice.

"Now—you will be a good little girl, my dear, and learn all that Cousin Norah has to teach you. I shall come and see you each year. Remember—that—I—am in your mother's place. And every month you will write me a letter."

Elsie looked at him solemnly.

"Yes, sir," she said.

He patted her hair, smiled at her docility, and went back to Italy and his epoch-making books.

Elsie was happy at Waddington. She was a shy and a sensitive child, and she allowed herself to be dominated by Miss Nimfrey's hard sentimentality, and she was not conscious of repression. The cottage had prim prettiness, a garden, and a little orchard, and there were two fields between it and the nearest of the Waddington houses. The country was beautiful, and Miss Nimfrey had one admirable passion, a love of wild flowers, insects and birds. In some ways she was wiser than she knew, for in cutting off Elsie from romping friendships with children of her own age, she supplied excellent compensations. Elsie was allowed puppies and kittens; she was given a piece of garden ground of her own, and was permitted to turn the summer-house into a corner of dreams. She was an imaginative child and her imagination was her companion in her games.

On Sundays Elsie and Miss Nimfrey went twice to Waddington church. It was their only dissipation, though once a month the curate's wife came to tea and brought her small daughter Evangeline with her. Evangeline and Elsie played games in the garden, held receptions in the summer-house, and discussed the future.

Evangeline was all for action.

"I'm going to drive a milk-cart when I grow up."

"And I," said Elsie, "am going to be a wife."

"Who's wife?"

"Mr. Parsloe's wife. Mother wished it."

Her receptivity had already accepted the inevitable without questioning it, for the figure of Jacob Parsloe had been erected above the altar of the child's life. Miss Nimfrey cherished the cult. Elsie was always hearing what a wonderful man Dr. Parsloe was, how learned, how good, how kind. Almost he had the impressiveness of Jehovah, and Elsie learned that he was a jealous god and expected little girls to be loving and obedient. Some day it might be her privilege to live with this great man and make a dutiful offering of herself in return for all that he had done for her.

Jacob Parsloe's books were kept in a special ebony book-slide on the mahogany table in Miss Nimfrey's drawing-room. She was very proud of them, somehow contriving to harmonize their new-world philosophy with her own prim orthodoxy. On several occasions Elsie possessed herself of one of Mr. Parsloe's books, and set herself to make his acquaintance under the cherry-tree on the small lawn at the back of the cottage. She began with the "Variations of Vitalism," and being unable to make head or tail of it, she was impressed by the great man's profundity. Inadvertently leaving the book on the grass while she indulged in a day dream, it was attacked and treated with scant reverence by Blot, her latest puppy. Blot found no difficulty in dealing with Mr. Parsloe's wisdom. He tore the book out of its cover, was castigated, and was the cause of Elsie's tearful departure to bed.

"What—would—Mr. Parsloe think of such carelessness?"

And Elsie realized that her god could be offended.

Each year Dr. Parsloe arrived from Italy and spent a fortnight in Waddington, staying at the "Mitre" in the village, where no one knew anything about him or his books. He took Elsie for walks, he catechized her, and he approved. From year to year the child saw little change in him; she was awed by his supposed greatness, by his size, by his rolling voice, by her own imagined debt to him. He represented duty, her mother, and the whole scheme of civilization. She was utterly innocent, and her happy docility had accepted all Miss Nimfrey's suggestive discipline.

She neither liked nor disliked Jacob Parsloe. It was not a question of liking.

He seemed to her as inevitable as the sky, or a sermon on Sunday, or her dinner, or the ending of winter by the spring.

As for Parsloe he approved.

"Norah, I congratulate you. I find Elsie both highly intelligent and obedient."

"And pretty," said his cousin; "the child is going to have looks."

Parsloe smiled faintly.

"Yes—I think she has a certain prettiness. Not too much mirror, my dear Norah; not too much mirror."

Elsie was fifteen when she became aware of a certain change in her great protector and friend. Arriving from Italy that year he looked at her with more distinct and active approval, with an appreciative glint of the eyes. He seemed kinder. He kissed her; he fondled her more than had been his custom, stroked her hair and pinched her cheek. Once when Miss Nimfrey happened to be out he took Elsie on his knees and talked to her with heavy yet menacing fondness.

"So my little girl is going to make me a good little wife."

"Yes, Mr. Jacob, I hope so," she said with gentle shyness.

"That's right, that's right."

In appearance, he had not changed, and Elsie saw no outward change in him, for she was far too much of a child to realize the nature of the man who had shut her up in a cage. Parsloe always had had eccentric tendencies, and he was growing more and more eccentric, more self-centred, more arrogant, more the old man in possession. He had offended all his old friends, for a man who has a savage sense of his own infallibility is not fit to have friends. He had begun to live like a hermit, shutting himself up with his own grandiloquent meditations. He was growing slovenly, careless, mean, and overbearing. His villa on the Italian coast was becoming an ogre's fortress in which he tore the flesh from the bones of other men's books, and indulged himself in savage scorns. Always he had been intolerant of criticism, and his vanity, living in select isolation, had grown like some rank and over-fed plant.

But how was a child to know all this? Miss Nimfrey may have suspected it, but she shut those thin lips of hers and did not interfere. She—too—had a grievance against the opposite sex, and her inverted spite took an almost sinister pleasure in cheating a young man for the benefit of an old one.

Yet even she was to have her moment of fear, of remorse and compassion. It happened before the marriage, when Elsie was eighteen. All the arrangements had been made: the banns had been put up for the first time in Waddington church; there had been shopping excursions to town; the buying of Elsie's trousseau. The wedding was to be a quiet one, and Parsloe and his young wife were leaving at once for Italy.

He loomed up like a big black bird, ready to pounce and to carry off something in his claws. He radiated a kind of menacing and hungry good humour, and for the first time in her life Elsie became conscious of him as something other than Dr. Jacob Parsloe. She felt a shrinking, a bewilderment, a fluttering of her wings against mysterious bars.

Three nights before the marriage, she appeared suddenly like a ghost in Miss Nimfrey's bedroom. She was in her nightdress, and her wonderful hair hung about her. She looked like a victim, and the elder woman's heart misgave her.

"Oh, Auntie, I'm frightened!"

She clung to the austere figure in the bed, and Miss Nimfrey tried to comfort her.

"Frightened, Elsie! Why, what is there to be frightened of?"

"I don't know. But is there anything——?"

"My dear, there is nothing for you to be afraid of. You are going to have a beautiful home, and a kind and distinguished husband."

"I know—I know—— But, oh—Auntie, it's all so strange!"

"There, there," said Miss Nimfrey; "all that shopping has over-excited you. Make up your mind to be happy and you—will—be happy."

CHAPTER III

On their way south the Parsloes stopped for two nights in Paris.

An Englishman who happened to travel in the same compartment with them in the train from Turin to Genoa was struck by the girl's attitude and expression. She seemed to shrink defensively into her corner. She did not speak. She had the appearance of having been surprised and overcome by some secret horror, and she was still dominated by it, and by the man who sat opposite her in the other corner. Her lids were red. She looked at him half furtively. When he spoke to her she seemed to give a sort of start, and to answer him coherently cost her an obvious effort.

The Englishman was interested in them both: in the girl's wedding-ring and new clothes, in her youth, her frightened bewilderment, and in her husband. This chance observer took a great dislike to

Parsloe. Not only was he far too old for the girl, but he did not appear to realize that it was necessary to treat her with great gentleness. He was a tyrannical, greedy person. The girl's frightened eyes seemed to annoy him; he was dissatisfied and impatient.

Once he spoke rather roughly to her.

"Come, come, now, why not look at the scenery? You have not seen Italy before."

The girl's eyes filled with tears. She said nothing; but she turned her face to the window, and held her handkerchief to her mouth.

Parsloe eyed her with obvious annoyance, and an air of ownership that was menacing.

As for the chance Englishman, he glanced at Parsloe with a look that said: "You—ought to be kicked."

It was autumn when Elsie Parsloe came to her new home, the Villa Pineta. She had her first glimpse of it as the carriage drove along the lovely coast from Santa Maria, with the cliffs and hills rising up on one side and the sea a blue sheet upon the other. She saw it as a square, grey, tower-like building standing on a headland above the sea. The flanks of the headland were almost precipitous, and covered above with a tangle of pines, ilexes, and wild olives. The carriage stopped outside the gate of the Villa Pineta, and Elsie saw it as a massive wooden door set in a stone wall that was twenty feet high, and this wall—carried across the narrow neck of the headland, isolated it completely.

Parsloe was watching her.

"My castle, my dear!" he said.

He rang the heavy bell, and the gate was opened by an Italian in blue trousers and a striped shirt, Luigi, the gardener, sixty-five years old. The luggage was carried in, the vetturino paid, and the gate closed on them. Elsie heard the carriage driving away to Santa Maria, and the jingling of the bell and the clatter of hoofs dying away under the cliffs left her with an added sense of loneliness.

She felt her husband's big hand on her shoulder.

"We are not disturbed here. And it is beautiful."

She was aware of something ironical in

him, a threatening and tyrannical fondness, the pressure of his hand forcing her gently up the broad path to the house. Beautiful indeed it was, this half wild garden on the headland floating above the sea, with the afternoon sunlight warming it, and the vine leaves turning to gold. Yet Elsie felt chilled, menaced. She shrank from the place as she had begun to shrink from the man. The shadows of tall cypresses fell across the path. Here and there a statue glimmered white in a mass of dusky foliage. There were flowers, rocks, cacti clinging to grey ledges, roses and climbing plants threading the trees and bushes, palms, orange trees with fruit upon them. She had glimpses of secret walks, the blue sea seen between the trunks of pines, a little round Classic temple half hidden by arbutus and box. It was beautiful, extraordinarily beautiful—and yet——!

They came to the house. Its tower-like face was reached by a broad flight of steps and entered by an arched doorway. An old woman waited at the top of the steps—an old woman, broad and squat, with a swarthy and expressionless face. To Elsie she looked like someone who had never been young.

Parsloe nodded at her.

"This—is Anna."

The woman's black eyes stared at Elsie, and she did not smile.

"Welcome, signora."

They entered the house. The tiled hall led into rooms which were huge, silent and lofty, and from their windows it was possible to drop a stone into the sea. Elsie could hear it murmuring and splashing on the grey-black rocks far below. The sound followed them everywhere, up the marble staircase to Parsloe's library, a room with a stone balcony jutting out into the blue. It was overwhelmed with books—this room; they ran up to the ceiling and lay in piles upon the floor. Near the window stood a knee-hole writing-desk.

"This—is where I work."

She had a feeling that he expected her to be impressed, but she was conscious only of feeling miserable, caged. And caged with him!

"What numbers of books," she said.

He patted her shoulder.

"Work—here—for my little wife. I want you to keep them dusted and in order. I want you to make a catalogue and an index. My Elsie is going to be very useful to me."

She had not a word to say, and her silence brought that frown to his forehead. His marriage had begun by disappointing him, in spite of Miss Nimfrey's years of discipline and Elsie's apparent docility. He remembered that first night with a shivering and shocked child sitting in her nightdress in the dark by the open window, dumb and terrified. He had been angry, sexually angry. It had seemed to him preposterous that she should have been shocked. Well, he would take steps to change all that!

"Come and see our rooms."

He swung her round and upstairs to the second floor, and here he showed her their bedroom, and a little room opening off it which he said she might consider as her very own. The furniture was Italian and made of walnut, and it looked heavy and ugly. Parsloe, standing in the middle of the bedroom, crushed her to him and forced a kiss.

She was cold as stone, but she did not resist.

"What a big house it is," she said. "Who does all the work?"

"Anna. But—of course—my dear—you will help. I believe in women working, even little women!"

His heavy playfulness was more frightening to her than his solemnity.

"Oh, yes—I will work," she faltered; "I like doing things about a house."

"Excellent," he said.

Later, she escaped into the garden and explored it, and behind all her exploration was the fear of a live thing shut up in a cage. She came to realize the nature of Parsloe's home. The high wall shut it off from the world, and she discovered that the gate was kept locked and that someone pocketed the key. The headland was completely isolated. There was one spot, a little narrow inlet with a steep path going down to it, which made the headland approachable from the sea, but Elsie did not discover that till later.

"I'm shut in here," she thought; "and there is no escape."

So her married life began, and if her

heart had cried out in her at the first shock of it, it soon ceased to rebel. Parsloe and the life of the Villa Pineta overwhelmed her, and in a little while she was accepting it all with a docility which had been instilled into her during the last six years. She was helpless and very unhappy, but in a little while she discovered that it was necessary to hide her unhappiness, for it made Parsloe angry. He flew into rages, and these rages of his terrified her. He was rough; he shouted; and once he made her hold out her hand and he struck at it savagely with a heavy ivory paper-knife.

"Oh, don't——! You have hurt me!"

"Learn to smile, and I shan't have to hurt you."

Slowly and systematically he crushed her both spiritually and physically, and she was such a little thing and so easily crushed. She became meek and dully consenting beneath the uxorious and jealous tyranny of this Jehovah of a husband. She had no experience to prove to her that as a husband he was not normal, and for years she had been overawed by the greatness of him, and fed upon Miss Nimfrey's anthems of praise. "I must be obedient and he won't frown at me."

The grieved male that was in Parsloe chuckled. He possessed a woman, a slave, a little dark-eyed, dutiful handmaid who waited upon his every whim.

Moreover, bully that he was, he felt secure. His orientalism sunned itself in a sense of its own cleverness. He had his Eve shut up in a garden where the only man thing was old Luigi, aged sixty-five, and there was no escape from the garden save by his—Jacob Parsloe's—consent. Once a month he would hire a carriage, and they would drive to Santa Maria or up into the hills to San Pietro. Elsie never went outside the gate without her husband, save to sit meekly beside him in the carriage, with a far away look in her eyes.

But life is cumulative, and all through that winter while Parsloe was teaching his caged bird to sing when he wished it, and to be silent when he commanded silence, he was laying up the seeds of punishment for himself. Like so many so-called great men, he was an overweening fool. His arrogance grew blind. He lived like a god in his retreat, a slovenly god who seemed to despise all the little fastidious things that matter. He was dirty; he would wear the same collar for a fortnight, and he shaved himself only when the spirit moved him. He had developed the continental habit of using a toothpick at meals, and he used it with an air of naked self-satisfaction. At night he would make Elsie stand behind his chair and stroke his hair with her little white fingers. He said it helped him to think.

By the time that the Spring came in she had begun to loathe him—though she was not acutely and actively conscious of her loathing, for she was too helplessly dumb and suppressed. The feeling was deep down in her under-consciousness, and was fed like some subterranean pool by slow percolation from the life above. Even the beauty of the world about her was in danger of growing ugly with the ugliness of this man's cruel selfishness.

She remembered sitting at the window of her little room one April day with the sea making a gentle murmur on the rocks below, a sea that was almost as blue as the sky above. She was conscious of a kind of anguish of yearning, for the world below her was full of the Spring. She had heard a peasant singing among the olive trees on the hills, the song a man sings when life is good and his heart is happy.

Her eyes filled with tears.

And then, suddenly, she was aware of that moving speck of colour out to sea, a blot of blurred crimson. She had to dry her eyes to look at it, to make sure that it was not a piece of colour in the rainbow of her tears.

She saw a boat with a crimson sail catching the sunlight out to sea, and somehow it pleased her, and she sat and watched it as a sick woman watches the play of sunlight on the walls of her room.

CHAPTER IV

ENGLISH people had taken the old Villa Andrea sunning itself in a green cleft of the hills about half a mile away along the coast. Their name was Lutterel, and the mother was an invalid, and yet not such an invalid that she had lost the joy of living. She had her son with her, a young man who had money of his own, who had taken "firsts" at Cambridge and was now a barrister-at-law.

"I think I'll play for six months, mater, before joining in the great scuffle."

Mary Lutterel loved him very dearly, for he was a rather lovable lad, but she loved him wisely and with the full knowledge of what a mother loses when she loves like a fool. She knew that some day she would lose him in the sense that he was hers, but that in losing she might win him and also a daughter.

They were quite happy together up at the Villa Andrea. Mary Lutterel read and lay in the sun, and painted a little, and dreamed of things that had been and of things that were to be. Geoffrey—or Geoff, as she called him—climbed the hills and sailed his boat which lay in the boat-house below in the little bay, and swam, for he was a great swimmer. His centre-board dinghy had a crimson sail.

The Lutterels may have heard of Jacob Parsloe, but that they knew anything of the inner life of the people on the head-land was wholly improbable, and all that happened afterwards was the product of coincidence.

Elsie was with Parsloe in his library one morning, copying out some notes for him. She had finished her piece of work, and while her husband was rummaging solemnly among some books she stepped out on to the stone balcony and looked down at the sea. A flaking of foam surrounded the headland, and here and there isolated black rocks pushed the blackness of their half-submerged backs through the swaying surface of the blue water. Elsie was watching the play of the sea when she became aware of some-thing else.

A man was swimming down there; she saw the movement of his head and the white play of his arms in the blue water. She was astonished; she stood very still, watching him, and saw him make for one of the basking rocks and climb out into the sunlight. He stood up; he was wearing a light blue bathing-dress, and she thought that he looked very tall and slim and graceful. His skin had a tinge of brown.

Suddenly, he glanced upwards and saw a girl on the distant balcony. The joy of the morning was in him, a happy, laughing exultation in the goodness of things and in his own strength. He waved a hand to her. Elsie waved back.

She saw him poised for a moment, and then he dived and began his passage homewards, keeping well out and away from the rocks. She continued to watch him. She had forgotten all about her solemn curmudgeon of a husband, and then she found him standing at her elbow.

"What on earth are you staring at, Elsie?"

For the first time in her life something within her resented that hectoring tone of his. She remembered, too, that he was short-sighted, though he would never allow that his sight had grown indifferent.

"Isn't it an octopus?" she said.

"Where?"

"Down there. Or perhaps——?"

He wrinkled up his forehead.

"Don't be silly," he said. "I fail to see anything."

She stared at him; she thought for the moment that he was being sly with her, for he had a ponderous slyness of his own; and then she realized that he could not see the swimmer out yonder.

She broke into laughter.

"How silly of me! I was sure that I saw an octopus. There are small ones, aren't there?"

"There are," he said; "but women see all sorts of absurd things—women and children."

She was to see the swimmer again, and many times, for the half-mile of water between the Villa Andrea boat-house and the headland gave young Lutterel both distance and a mark to aim at. His choosing of the headland had had no other significance, but the tower-like house perched up yonder and the girl's figure on the balcony were certain to provoke conjectures. He knew that Dr. Jacob Parsloe lived there, "The Learned Englishman," as the Italians called him, and Lutterel had read one of Parsloe's books. It would have bored him, had not its arrogance and its scorn for most other thinkers provoked the intellectual antagonism of a young man who hated all priggery, intellectual or otherwise. He supposed the girl on the balcony to be Parsloe's daughter, and so natural was the assumption that it was never corrected until other impulses had been born.

Sometimes he would sit and bask on one of the rocks, but only once again did he see the girl; but she saw him, and the figure of the swimmer tantalized her. He seemed so free, so strong, so much the master of all that world of sea and sky and air, while she was cooped up, with all the youth in her suppressed. It was very natural that the figure of the swimmer should come to be symbolical, a challenge to that in her which was alive yet sleeping. The woman in her stirred—the girl-woman waiting for her mate.

"I wonder who he is?" she thought.

"It must be lonely for a girl—there," was his reflection.

"I suppose I shall never know who he is, and never see him any nearer," she decided.

"I wonder what sort of daughter a man like Parsloe would have?"

Each assumed that the other was no more than a passing cloud-shadow over the sea, and so it might have been but for the south-west wind. It blew hard one morning, and Elsie, idling in the garden, saw the cypress tops bent like sickles. The sea was a hard blue, and ridged with white horses, and on the hills the ruffled olives showed the grey under-lining of their leaves.

"It is too rough for him to swim this morning," she thought.

She came down through a little thicket of pines to where a terraced walk ran along the edge of the cliff, and as she reached the walk she saw her swimmer there beyond the point. She was astonished, and a moment later she was afraid, for even to her inexperienced eyes it seemed that all was not well with him. He had dared the rough sea beyond the point where the headland gave no shelter, but he had turned about and was fighting his way back, and making very little progress. Sometimes she lost sight of him for a moment, and she held her breath. Slowly, but very slowly, he made towards the headland and the comparatively calm water under the lee of it.

He gained it. She saw him right below her, and she realized that he was swimming very feebly. He was exhausted. He turned on his back and floated, in order to rest, but the set of the current began to drift him away from the land. He struck out again, and Elsie realized that he was trying to reach the rocks below her, and in realizing it she remembered that the cliffs dropped into the water like a well, save at one place where there was a cleft in them and a steep path went down to a tiny inlet. She wondered whether he knew of it, whether he would find it.

She ran. She reached the rough path and scrambled down it, and when she was halfway down it she had a sudden, vivid picture of him floating in the blue-green water framed by the grey walls of the cleft. He was about twenty yards from the shore, almost motionless, his head half submerged, his arms moving feebly. She paused there, holding to the stem of a shrub, horrified by the thought that he was going to sink under her very eyes.

She scrambled on, calling to him.

"Here—here—swim this way."

Her voice must have roused a last effort in him, for he half raised his head, and making a few spasmodic strokes, he managed to reach the shallow water, but here his strength failed him and he collapsed within a yard or two of the shore. There was a patch of rough shingle here, and he lay on it with the water washing over him. Elsie had reached the bottom of the path. She realized that he might drown even in that shallow water.

She splashed her way down to him, got her hands under his shoulders, and dragged him towards safety. He had not lost consciousness completely, and he was able to help himself and her, and when she rolled a boulder forward with one foot and put it under his head, he spread his arms with an air of exhausted and consenting relief and lay still.

But soon he was sitting up, and smiling at her.

"I say, that was a near thing! If it had not been for you——"

She smiled back at him, strangely moved by his English voice. They were a little shy of each other, these two, and with that quick shyness which often is part of a swift, mutual liking.

He glanced at her wet feet and skirt.

"I'm sorry——"

"But I'm not," she said; "it was lucky that I saw you."

"It was. I shall remember."

He stood up; he was a little shaky but smiling, and she thought how straight and clean his eyes were. He, too, was filled with a sudden sense of her delicate and gentle comeliness. She was his type in voice, eyes, figure, skin and hair.

"I say, you ought to go and change those wet things."

She flushed, for it was a new thing for her to be considered.

"But you?"

"Oh, I'm quite all right now. I have been just as badly cooked in the "Mays" at Cambridge, and forgotten all about it five minutes afterwards. I shall just drop back into the sea and swim to that point there where the road runs above the beach. I can do a sprint home."

"Is it quite safe?" she asked.

He looked with sudden attentiveness into the brown solemnity of her eyes.

"Oh, quite. Please don't worry. I'm most awfully grateful to you. By the way, my name is Lutterel, Geoffrey Lutterel; my mother and I have the Villa Andrea along there."

"And my name is——"

"Oh, I know that," he said with a quick smile; "or at least—part of it. Mr. Parsloe is a celebrity."

"Elsie is the other part."

He repeated it—"Elsie," and it was obvious that it pleased him. They looked at each other with significant and momentary intentness, and then he wandered out, and turning before he plunged, waved a hand.

"I suppose you were here before we

were. If you would come and call on my mother—I know she would be delighted. She is an invalid."

"Dr. Parsloe never calls on anyone," she said.

His face expressed faint surprise.

"I see. I expect he is too big to bother about formalities. But—the sea has introduced us."

She nodded, and watched him swim along under the cliff till he reached the stretch of shore below the road. From the roadway he turned and looked back, and seeing her still standing there, waved a hand.

"Ought I to tell?" she thought as she climbed the path; "no, I won't tell. Surely I have a right to just one little secret of my own."

Lutterel, trotting barefooted along the lonely road, smiled at his own thoughts.

"Who would thought that a pedant like Parsloe would have had that girl for a daughter!"

CHAPTER V

As Lutterel had put it, "The sea has introduced us," and the sea became the inevitable pathway, the way of fate between these two.

Mary Lutterel heard of the adventure, and from the way he spoke of it she knew that though he had escaped the sea, he had been captured by something else, the set of a girl's head, the way she looked, the light behind her eyes.

She met the situation resignedly, knowing that a generously opened door is less provoking than one that is kept shut.

"Why not ask Miss Parsloe to call? I should like to write and thank her."

"Parsloe is not a social light, mater."

"But the girl——?"

"I think she is rather shy."

His mother knew that this shyness pleased him.

The rough weather continued for two days, and it rained as it can rain in the south, but when the south-west wind died away, and the sea became a great turquoise under the spring sky, the hunter went forth to his hunting. He got out his dinghy from under the overhanging shade of the ilexes and pines, and sculling out of the narrow bay, set a course for the headland. The wind was very light and off the shore, but someone on the headland saw the crimson sail.

She stood there on the balcony of Parsloe's room, knowing that the room was empty, and that the heavy presence had left it. Dr. Parsloe had gone to Rome to buy books and to attend some symposium of the learned, and he would remain in Rome ten days. Ten precious, unshadowed days!

The crimson sail came nearer. She watched it, conscious of the drift of some new meaning into her life, half guessing that the man who steered that boat steered it with a purpose. In a little while it was off the headland and lying close below her. Lutterel stood up. He shouted something, raised his hat and pointed towards the place where she had rescued him.

She could not catch his words, but his meaning was in her heart.

Should she go down? For in that instant of time she knew what her going down would signify. Youth called, and she stood there trembling to the bird-note of her own desire. Should she go? And then her own youth carried her away, blindly and yet not blindly. She knew, she fore-saw, she fore-felt. There was wilfulness in her going, a cry of revolt, a reaching-out to that joy and anguish which had been denied her. She felt somehow that she was throwing herself from a height into the sea, and that life was like that, inevitable, sacrificial.

Lutterel had run the boat aground on the little strip of shingle and he sprang out to meet her. She knew at once by the look in his eyes what had made him come.

"I want to thank you again. By the way, my mother is writing to you. She would like to meet you and Dr. Parsloe."

She flushed, a soft kindling colour under her white skin.

"Dr. Parsloe has gone to Rome."

"But you——?" he asked; "why shouldn't I take you back to lunch?"

She hesitated, having her own inward reasons for not wishing to meet another woman and that woman—his mother.

"Dr. Parsloe won't let me—— I mean —he prefers solitude."

He was surprised, a little puzzled, but he was very quick in sensing a delicate shade of feeling, and he abandoned the argument. But he had another suggestion to make.

"Mayn't I take you for a sail?"

"I should love it."

He handed her into the boat, and in entering it she knew that she was beginning a voyage upon a strange and hazardous sea.

Lutterel went back to the Villa Andrea, and during lunch he made some sort of confession to his mother.

"I don't think I should send that letter, mater."

Her eyes, waited, asking a question.

"She seemed a little unhappy at the idea. I haven't quite got the situation. There is something queer in the life there."

"Eccentricities?"

"My feeling is that Parsloe is an old

man of the sea A tyrant. I could gather that from the stuff he writes."

"He believes in the protected daughter!"

"That is for me to find out."

He was off the headland again next day, and on the day after that, and when once love had descended the path, it learns to descend it blindfold. It was not that Elsie did not care; she had begun to care so much that she braved further caring. Life had come to her, surprising, poignant and wonderful. She had not asked for it; she had not suspected its passionate appeal; but now that it had come she clung to it with sudden desperate happiness. Why should she not be happy for a week? She knew now how greatly Jacob Parsloe had sinned against her innocence. Moreover, the awakened woman in her knew that she would never forgive him.

The sea was still, and the sun shone. She looked into the man's eyes, and he into hers.

"I say—I should like to teach you to swim."

"But I have no dress."

"I'll buy one at Santa Maria."

He bought the dress, and she changed her clothes in the little classic temple and went down to him with her bronze hair blowing, and her limbs white as her throat. She saw his eyes. She was so beautiful to him that he was awed.

"Elsie, you are——"

She gave him one dear, veiled look, half confused, half exultant.

"I promise not to be frightened."

"As if I could do anything to make you afraid!"

She learnt in two lessons. At the end of a week she could swim out to one of the rocks beyond the headland, and Anna saw them there, and Elsie knew that she was seen. She did not care. And then, suddenly, she began to care. It came upon her abruptly with the realization of the amazing fact that he believed that she was Parsloe's daughter.

She discovered it quite casually, and the discovery distracted her. How had it come about? She remembered that they had always treated Parsloe as an impersonal figure; that she had never spoken of him as her husband, and that Lutterel had never referred to him as her father. She felt her very soul quivering in its fragile shell.

"I shall have to tell him," she thought; "I must tell him before—he—comes back."

But what effect would the truth have upon Lutterel? Would he hate her? Would he think that she had deceived him? Would not all the glamour go? Was it fair to him to leave him dreaming even for one other day?

She had taken off her wedding ring and hidden it on that first morning, not because she had wished to deceive, but rather as a symbolical act, a putting off from her of that other man's memory. She regretted it, and on that eighth morning she went down to the sea with the ring upon her finger.

"Two more days, two more days," was her inward cry, "and I am killing them!"

Lutterel was waiting for her, and together they swam out to one of the rocks. He had not noticed that hoop of gold, but he was aware of the shadow upon her, the darkness of her veiled eyes. "What ails you?" he thought, with a love that hovered.

He reached the rock first, and climbing out knelt down to help her up. She gave him one hand, the hand with the ring on it, and he saw it. She could feel the sudden pause in him, that moment of rigidity, as though the full action of life had stopped. He helped her out. They sat down side by side in the sun. He was silent, and stealing a glance at him, she saw his eyes.

And suddenly, she laid a hand on his, her other hand, for that silence was not to be borne.

"Geoff, I thought you knew! It was only yesterday——"

He did not look at her.

"Then, he is——?"

"Yes, my husband."

"Good God!" he said, and sat staring.

She began to tremble even in the warm Italian sunlight, and she could not control that quivering of her limbs. He felt it. The vibration spread to him, but not passively, for his was a man's trembling before the crisis of an impassioned act.

"Elsie——"

He put an arm round her.

"What made you——? Yes, you must tell me. I've got to know."

She hid her face.

"Don't——! I can't bear it. O, Geoff, I wish I were dead!"

From that moment his love took charge of her; he was very gentle yet very masterful, for that cry of hers had gone to his heart.

"Elsie, we can't talk here, and I must talk to you. Come."

He dropped back into the sea and drew her gently after him, and side by side they swam back slowly to the cleft in the cliffs. She hung her head and stood miserable and submissive.

"What do you want me to do?"

"You are coming out in the boat with me, Elsie. Go and change; I'll change here."

She went, and in little while she returned to him, drooping, heavy-eyed and pale.

"I've hurt you, Geoff," she said.

"I'm thinking of you," he answered.

They put out to sea, and Lutterel hoisted the sail, but when they were a mile from the coast he lowered the sail and let the boat drift on the calm water. They sat side by side in the stern sheets, hands clasped, heads together.

"Now, you will tell me everything. I love you, and I have a right to know."

She told him the history of her life, from the day when Jacob Parsloe had come to the house where her mother lay dying.

Neither of them knew of that carriage trundling along the coast road from Santa Maria, or guessed that Parsloe had returned before his time. He arrived. Luigi opened the gate for him and carried in his bag, and at the top of the steps leading into the house Parsloe found Anna waiting for him, the sinister and inscrutable Anna who never smiled.

"Where is the signora?"

She looked at him with a grim curiosity that had an element of contempt.

"She is not here, signor."

"Not here!"

"No; she is in a boat with a young man."

Anna turned about and entered the house, and Parsloe followed her. She went to one of the seaward windows of the dining-room and pointed.

"Out there. Every day they swim together. I have watched them with the opera glasses. He is a very handsome young man."

Parsloe, the philosopher, cursed her.

"Damn you, where are the glasses? Why didn't you send me word?"

"The glasses are on the table in your library, signor."

He rushed upstairs with a kind of blundering fury. He sat down in a chair by the window with the glasses in his hands.

Dusk was falling, a warm, April dusk, when Lutterel climbed the path from the boat-house to the garden of the Villa Andrea. It was full of perfumes, this garden; full of sad silences; and as he went up through the thickets and under the pergola, with its vines and roses and wisteria, he remembered the lips that he had kissed. His mother was on the terrace, lying in her long chair. She smiled at him as he came to her in the dusk, and then her smile died away.

He stood quite still, looking out towards the sea.

"Geoff," she said very softly.

She saw his head go up with a movement of defiance, defiance of life, not of her. He walked to the balustrade. When he spoke his voice had a fierce tenderness behind it.

"She's Parsloe's wife."

There was a short pause between each of his tense sentences.

"He's a beast to her. She's unhappy. He adopted her when she was quite a kiddie, had her drilled and disciplined into the idea of marrying him. She was utterly innocent. He kept her a child, hidden away with some damned female relation of his, and then—he married her. He is somewhere over fifty, and she's nineteen."

His mother lay very still.

"Poor Geoff," she said.

He faced about suddenly, and when she looked at him she knew that the first tragedy had come into his life.

"I could kill that man," he said.

She held out a hand to him.

"Geoff, dear, be kind—to her—and to yourself. Don't see her again."

"I—must—see her again," he said.

CHAPTER VI

ELSIE, climbing the path with Lutterel's kisses fresh upon her face, was taken unawares by the man who was waiting for her by the wall on the edge of the cliff. He had been leaning upon it, listening to the voices below, and to the splash of Lutterel's sculls as he pulled away.

"I presume that you have enjoyed yourself!"

She stood very still, a little, desolate figure looking up with frightened eyes into his ominous face.

"I did not know you were back."

"Obviously!" he said, and laughed; and that laugh of his shocked her.

He made no attempt to touch her, but she felt his bulk overshadowing her with the menace of things physical.

"Who is the young gentleman?"

She held her breath.

"I shan't tell you."

He bent over her.

"Oh, you won't! Well, I'll find out, if necessary. But I don't think that it will be necessary."

Her little flash of defiance died away. He leaned against the wall with his back to it and his arms resting on the stone coping, and observed her with ugly and savage intentness. He sneered.

"All women are alike. Even a child like you, ready to be fooled and to fool."

She hung her head.

"It was you who did the first wrong—in marrying me."

"Oh, did I!" he snarled.

"Yes, I didn't know. You kept me in ignorance of everything. You——"

"I saved you from a kitchen or the gutter, my dear."

"I wish you had left me there," she said.

His anger grew thunderous.

"That's gratitude! A man may do everything for a girl, but when some twopenny halfpenny boy turns up she forgets all her promises. But clear your mind of all that nonsense. I married you, and I'm your husband."

He caught her by the arm.

"Come along. I'll give you a lesson. I'll teach you to whom you belong."

She did not resist, for she was too overwhelmed and too miserable, nor had she divined the complete cruelty of his purpose. He led her into the house where the daylight was growing dim. She turned instinctively towards the dining-room, and blundering against him and his opposing purpose, was pushed towards the stairs. They climbed the first flight, and she imagined that he was taking her to the balcony to scold her like some super-schoolmaster, but they passed the library door, and then—she understood.

"No, no, not up there!"

They were at the foot of the second flight, and she hung back, pleading.

"No, no, oh—please——"

He jerked her savagely by the arm.

"Come on."

"No, no, Jacob—you can't—you——"

She began to struggle, and her struggles enraged him. The veins stood out on his forehead. She was aware of his big white face hanging even as he picked her up in his arms and carried her to their room. She ceased to struggle, but made a little moaning appeal.

"Oh, don't——! It's not right; it's horrible. I don't love you. Jacob, please kill me, but not that!"

He had no pity.

"You shall learn," he said.

When he left her she remained for a long while with her face buried in the pillow, making no sound, and lying quite still. The room grew dark, but it was less dark than her thoughts. For this man had taken her love and crushed it, covered it with shame, and left it broken and humiliated. She loathed him. He had become a horror to her, a thing of savage and brutal baseness.

Presently she shivered and stood up, and going to the window, drooped there with her face towards the sea. She could distinguish the dim shapes of the rocks where she and Lutterel had swum together and sat dreaming in the sunlight.

A great pang shot through her.

"My mate, my life's mate," she said in a whisper, "this man has made me—not fit for you."

She felt a horror of herself. She wanted

to efface the strain of it, to forget, to die.

"I can't go on living" she thought. "I can't—I can't."

She stroked the window ledge with the tips of pensive and caressing fingers.

"No, not from here, not from this window."

Her purpose took shape. She crossed softly towards the door, and feeling for the lock, found that the key was on the inside and the door unlocked. She crept out and down the stairs, but below her she saw an oblong patch of light, the open doorway of the library where Parsloe's lamp had been lit. She thought to slip by it unnoticed, but as she passed the doorway she heard his voice.

"Elsie, come here——."

She fled, only to hear him following her down the stairs, and she could feel them shaking with his angry, blundering weight. The garden door was shut, but she got it open. Parsloe had reached the foot of the stairs.

"Stop!" he said.

But she was out in the soft, April darkness, and running for the terrace where the drop was almost sheer to the rocks below, and she would have cheated him and died that night if she had not stumbled over a fir root and fallen. She reached the wall and was lifting herself over it when Parsloe caught her and dragged her back.

She struggled with him.

"Don't—don't! Oh, let me die, Jacob. I want to die."

He dragged her, weeping, back to the house.

"You little fool," he said; "I suppose I shall have to shut you up until your sanity returns."

CHAPTER VII

About nine o'clock next morning Lutterel grounded his boat in the inlet and stood watching the path. It was a perfect day, with the water lying like blue green glass above the dark patterning of the submerged rocks, and the tops of the pines above giving a more intense blue to the sky. The soft lapping of the sea made the boat grind gently on the shingle.

Lutterel waited for an hour, but no Elsie appeared upon the path. He sat in the stern sheets, he tramped about the strip of shingle, pulling out eventually to the rocks beyond the headland, and hoping to see her on the balcony. All that he saw was the woman Anna shaking a red rug from one of the windows.

He returned to the inlet, drew the dinghy well up on the shingle, and dared the path. His feeling was that Elsie was in hiding after the happenings of yesterday, that she was full of self reproaches, that she shirked facing the dear anguish of another day.

"I must see her," was his thought.

He reached the top of the path, rounded the rough stone pillar in which the wall ended, and came plump upon Parsloe who had been waiting for him there.

They looked at each other, and Lutterel knew why Elsie remained invisible. He saw her tragedy in Parsloe's heavy and threatening face.

They explained nothing; they justified nothing. The war between them was instant and open.

"I suggest that you keep your hands off other people's property."

"I did not know that she was your wife—till yesterday."

"So she fooled the lover as well as the husband. You need not worry. I think I am capable of making her regret it."

He stood there in all his arrogant clumsiness, a man prematurely aged, with the arteries knotted on his sallow temples. To Lutterel he was a creature of sacrilegious fat, of ungainly and looming anger.

"You were a cad to marry her."

"Indeed! But I—am—married to her, my young friend. Your hanging about here will hurt her more than it will hurt me or you."

They were very near to blows, but

Lutterel controlled himself, while the love in him hardened to fine steel.

"I might gather that—from the look of you. Good God! how I should hate you—if I——"

He saw the sullen blaze in Parsloe's eyes and turned back to the path to escape from the thought of killing. There was tenderness, a wild compassion at the back of his man's rage. For every word he uttered this other man would make her pay.

"Damn him!" he thought as he went down to the boat, "damn him; he shan't hurt her—if I can help it."

Lutterel did not look back, and if he had he would not have seen the other man leaning against the wall as though he had suddenly felt giddy. Parsloe's face was the colour of clay. His big, loose mouth with its flabby pinkness, was all awry. His eyes stared. He seemed to be listening to something that had happened inside himself. His lips moved. He stood up and away from the wall.

"I'm all right," he said to himself, "quite all right. I could have thrown that young brute into the sea."

Lutterel went back to the Villa Andrea.

"I've seen him," he said, "and I understand."

He sat sideways on the coping of the balustrade, looking towards the headland, while his mother pleaded for him, for herself, and for the girl.

"We'll go away, Geoff. You know how impossible such things are. Sometimes—when we break we can't mend."

"I mean to break—and mend."

"O, my dear!"

He went to her quickly, and kneeling down behind her chair, put his hands over her shoulders.

"Mater, I'd do most things for you; you know I would. But I won't leave her there—to that. I can't."

"It's a blind alley, dear."

"I'll face that. I must face it. Mater, will you stay here or will you go?"

She lay very still awhile, suffering and thinking.

"I think I'll go to Florence, Geoff. The Harkers are there. Will you take me to Florence?"

He nodded.

"But I shall have to come back. That's understood, mater?"

"Oh, my dear," she said, "if I could have saved you this!"

"But you couldn't," he answered her; "it has happened; perhaps it was meant to happen. Life must be like that."

So the Lutterels went to Florence, and Parsloe—who had made it his business to know something about the people at the Villa Andrea, was able to tell Elsie that her lover had gone away. He was keeping her locked in one of the lower rooms which had a huge old rusty grid over its window, giving her to understand that she would remain shut up there like a naughty child until she saw fit to behave as a wife and a reasonable being.

He meant to subdue her, and to so humiliate her that she should become the meek slave he coveted. This emotional experience might be turned to good account. He would so handle it that she would not need another.

The empty Villa Andrea gave him the chance to be superior and sneering. He gloated over the telling of its emptiness, nor was he wholly truthful.

"That is what your pup is worth. He

has run away and forgotten. I think I frightened him a little."

She sat and watched Parsloe with solemn and expressionless eyes.

"He saw you?"

"I met him on your favourite path, my dear Elsie, and he went down it in rather a hurry. You can rely on my promise that he will never come back."

She did not believe him. She could not have explained to Parsloe why she did not believe him, but she didn't. There were things that he would never understand.

But she felt very hopeless and weak, like one who has been sick, and who lacks the will either to die or to live. Her attitude to life was one of lassitude and apathy; she ceased to react; she ceased to care very much what happened.

One day she asked Parsloe to let her go out into the garden.

"Yes," he said, "if you promise—promise to be a good girl—and sensible."

"Oh—I promise," she said wearily.

It was the first sign of surrender, and his owl's face beamed with complacency. He even patted her shoulder and made as though to draw her to him, but feeling her stiff young body straining away from his he had the sense to temporize. Now that she had put herself on the right path, a little humouring of her might be allowable.

"Go and get some fresh air, my dear. And to-morrow—perhaps—we will order the carriage."

She went out and sat listlessly in the sunshine, thinking how a whole age seemed to have passed over the earth since last she drove with her husband in that carriage.

At the end of a week, with the Villa Andrea remaining empty, and Elsie sinking deeper and deeper into a listless acquiescence, Jacob Parsloe felt himself triumphant. He grew careless. He began to regard his wife's love affair as the mere escapade of a child, and to believe that Lutterel had been no more serious than a boy amusing himself in someone else's orchard. He did not know that Lutterel was staying at an hotel in Santa Maria, and that he walked after dark to the Villa Andrea boat-house.

Lutterel was in the garden each night, waiting for his chance to speak with Elsie, and in time that chance came.

The moon was up, but Parsloe had never been a moon-man, and the lamp in the library shone on the heavy pallor of his face. Elsie had wandered out, and she was going towards the little classic temple at the end of the cypress walk when Lutterel came out from behind one of the trees.

"Elsie. Don't be afraid."

She gave a little cry of anguish and of joy.

"Geoff!"

"My darling!"

And then, to his great amazement, she leaned against one of the cypresses, clasping the bole and hiding her face against it.

"Don't touch me, dear; I'm—I'm not fit to be touched by you."

"Elsie——!"

"No, no, he has made me——"

He felt the trembling of her, the sobbing breath in her throat, and his love would not be held off.

"Elsie. Tell me, anything, everything."

"I can't," she said.

"Oh, my dear, don't you know that you can tell me anything. I love you."

His arms were the compelling and tender arms of a lover, and she could not hold out against him. She put up her face to be kissed, and then hid herself in him and against him.

"Geoff, he has been horrible to me."

"My darling! Tell me."

She felt him stiffen, felt his arms tighten about her. It was the anger of the lover: a generous and fierce anger, full of compassion and scorn. He pressed his lips against her hair.

"That settles it," he said; "you are coming away with me."

"Oh, Geoff, I daren't."

"But I dare. You are coming away with me for ever and ever, away from all this. You must."

It took him an hour to persuade her, but when he left her she had promised to meet him at nine o'clock the following night. He was going back to Santa Maria to make arrangements and buy tickets. They would catch the night train for Genoa and Paris.

CHAPTER VIII

SOME time next morning Luigi told Parsloe that a man had taken a boat out of the Villa Andrea boat-house on the previous night.

"I think it was the young Inglese, signor. I could not go too close for fear he might hear or see."

Parsloe raged, but his rage was an inward rage, and the beast in him grew cunning. He let the day pass as though there were no cloud in the sky, but he spent it in watching Elsie for any sign of secret fear.

At lunch, and with an air of almost genial playfulness, he suggested that they should order the carriage that evening and go to dine at Santa Maria. He observed her narrowly, and he noticed the frightened clouding of her eyes. She was too sensitive, too tremulous with suppressed emotion, to meet him with a face of brass.

"I'm rather tired. Another night."

He let the matter drop, but his savage jealousy grew more sure.

"Very well, my dear," and he smiled, "we will spend a little quiet evening at home. Just you and I."

She was frightened. It hurt her to deceive him, perhaps because she loathed him so thoroughly; the whole business made her feel sordid and horrible. But did he suspect? She dared not think of what might happen if he suspected, and she clung desperately to the prospect of her flight. She longed for it now with all youth's passion for sincerity. It would be a clean act, wholesome, and final, and it would put an end to this gross make-believe.

She was agitated, overstrung. She dared not remain near him, and she spent the afternoon lying on the couch in her room, pretending that she had a headache.

At dinner Parsloe was almost jocose, and for a little while she was deceived by his playfulness, but before the meal was over he had begun his dagger thrusts. He tortured her, and she flinched before him.

"A beautiful night, my dear. I suggest that we sit in the garden and look at the moon."

"I think I shall go to bed," she faltered.

She realized that he was watching her with eyes of mockery and of menace.

"Oh, nonsense. Now—if I were a young man!"

"Please, I'm so tired."

"I see," he said, "I see. I must take care that you do not overtire yourself to-night."

At the end of the meal he rose with an air of looming grimness, and held out his arm.

"Come upstairs to the library. I'll read to you."

She went. She began to be possessed by the horror of the knowledge that he knew, and that he was playing some monstrous game with her. The lamp had been lit in the library. He followed her in and locked the door, and put the key in his pocket.

He knew.

She sat down in a chair, while he remained standing by the table. She knew that the crisis had come, and something in her bade her resist, struggle, make one fight against the looming and arrogant mass of his tyranny. She noticed that there was a stick lying on the table, and that the windows to the balcony were open.

"Jacob," she said, "please unlock that door."

She was astonished at the level quietness of her own voice.

"Why?"

She looked him straight in the eyes.

"I am going away—with him."

"You think so!"

"Please," she said, "if I don't go I shall die."

She had seen him angry, but never such anger as she saw now. His face seemed to swell up, its mouth wide open, its eyes like dull glass. He roared at her; he picked up the stick which lay on the table.

She sprang up as he clutched at her. An overturned chair lay between them, and suddenly she saw the furious figure falter as though something had broken within it. Its face grew flaccid. It made a groping gesture with one hand, searching for the table, rested for the moment with fingers spread upon it, and then fell sideways. It seemed to crumple up; it slipped to the floor.

She stood staring. Then she stooped over him, felt for the key, and finding it, unlocked the door and fled down the stairs.

"Anna," she called, "Anna."

The woman's face showed below.

"Anna—the signor is ill; he has had a fit or something; come and help me."

Together they returned to the room, and between them they lifted Parsloe and laid him on the sofa. He was conscious, but paralysed; he made some sort of noise in his throat; he kept blinking his eyes at them; his face was all drawn to one side.

"It is a fit, signora."

Elsie was standing between the lamp and the door, and as she made a movement towards the door she found Parsloe's eyes fixed on her. They were full of intelligence, and they had become soft, agonized, questioning. She understood. He thought that she was going to her lover, that she was deserting him even as he deserved to be deserted.

She covered her face and went out.

"I have killed him," she thought, "and in his way he must have loved me."

She went unsteadily down the stairs and out into the moonlit garden, and when Lutterel met her she fell into his arms and clung to him.

"Oh, Geoff, Geoff, he has had a stroke; he is dying. I told him—I told him——"

She was beyond herself, and he carried her to a stone seat and held her as though she were a child.

"You told him!"

"Yes—I think he knew. I told him that I should die if I did not go away with you, and then he raged at me. And suddenly—he fell down. He is paralysed."

He rocked her in his arms.

"Poor Elsie; poor darling."

But in a little while her soul came back to her. She broke gently from him and sat beside him on the seat, very solemn and pale, her eyes looking straight out over the sea.

"Geoff," she said, "do you understand? Can—you understand?"

"Tell me."

"That—I can't leave him now. I don't

know why, but that is how I feel. He has been horrible to me, and now he is helpless. Oh, how life hurts one!"

He put an arm gently about her neck and drew her head so that it lay against his cheek.

"What do you want me to do, Elsie?"

"Take your boat and go for a doctor."

"I'll go," he said.

Dull, driven by a strange sense of the inevitable, she returned to the house and the library where Anna was sitting on a chair beside the sofa. She was instantly conscious of Parsloe's eyes. They watched her enter the room; they expressed astonishment, and something more than astonishment. She knew that he had not expected to see her again.

She approached the couch.

"I have sent for the doctor. Do you understand?"

He blinked his eyelids, and she understood that it meant "yes," and sitting down near him, she folded her hands in her lap and waited.

CHAPTER IX

THE doctor came about midnight. He was a Lombard: tall, serious, with a fine head and quiet eyes. Elsie stood beside him while he examined her husband and made a diagnosis that was almost self-evident.

"How old is he?" he asked.

"I don't know," she answered; "sixty, perhaps. He never told me."

The Lombard drew her aside on to the balcony and began to speak in his gentle, pleasant voice.

"You understand Italian—yes? It is a case of cerebral bleeding, bleeding into the brain. You understand?"

She nodded.

"He must not be moved. You will have to put up a bed in this room; he must have plenty of pillows. You will need a nurse."

"I will nurse him," she said.

"Signora, such cases are not easy; he is a heavy man."

"The woman will help me."

There was a short silence between them, while the Lombard stroked his short beard and looked at the stars and the sea. He felt that the figure beside him was trying to ask him a question; he glanced at her; he saw her lips move. He divined what she wanted to ask him.

"I do not know yet. To-morrow—perhaps—I shall be able to tell."

She bent her head.

"He will never be——?"

"No—he will never be the same. If he lives some power may come back, how much I cannot say. He may not be able to speak. It is right that you should be told."

"Thank you," she said; "thank you."

He moved back into the room, stood looking at Parsloe for some seconds, nodded at him kindly and turned towards the door. Elsie followed him; his eyes had told her that he had more to say to her; and she went with him down the stairs.

"I will come early to-morrow morning.

I shall bring what is necessary. There are certain dangers which you will have to guard against."

"Please tell me."

He gave her simple directions for the nursing of such a case, bowed to her with natural dignity, and left her to face a dimly foreshadowed martyrdom.

But first she went to the head of the path leading to the inlet, and here she found Lutterel waiting in the moonlight. She felt a sudden passionate pity for him, far more pity than she felt for herself.

"Poor Geoff, you must be so tired."

She was very calm, and her calmness dominated him. She seemed to have drawn apart, and sensitively he understood that she was not to be touched.

"How is he?"

"It is a paralytic stroke. He may recover; he may not. The doctor cannot tell me yet."

He heard the sound of her breathing.

"Geoff, I must stay. Come to me—to-morrow. Oh, try to understand."

He bent and kissed one of her hands.

"Elsie—I understand. God bless you."

Sleep was very far from her, and when

hey had done all that could be done, she
ent Anna to bed.

"I shall watch. If I need you I will
all you."

She knew that the woman's sullen eyes
ccused her of having caused this tragedy,
ut she was not hurt by the injustice of the
ccusation, for she had chosen to sit by
his heavily breathing body of a living
eath. What greater restitution could she
nake?

To remain, watched by those helpless
yes, held there by some instinct which she
id not question though it caused her a dull
nguish! She sat through those slow hours,
ometimes rising to moisten Parsloe's lips
r to raise his head upon the pile of pillows.
he shrank from him; it cost her an effort
o touch him, and yet she did it.

"How strange!" she thought; "how little
e can foresee what will happen within
urselves! I give up everything—for
hat?"

She had begun by sitting near the
indow where Parsloe could not see her,
ut soon she became aware that he was
estless. He made queer noises, like a
umb beast, trying to make itself under-

stood. She rose, and moved her chair
that he could see her.

"Is that what you wish?"

He blinked his eyes. He wanted to lo
at her, but she began to realize that
looked at her in a different way, not as t
bully and the possessor, but more like
child. A pang shot through her. Th
look of his seemed to doom her to anoth
sort of slavery.

Yet she acquiesced, feeling the inevitabl
ness of her acquiescence, and when t
dawn came she spoke to him gently a
went out into the garden. She watch
the sun come up over the sea, thinking
she watched it that one can never be su
of what another dawn will bring, and ho
different the reality may be from t
reality of our dreams. She should ha
been with that other man, her love
gliding northwards to the green of
English spring.

She bowed her head. She was ve
weary, and yet she knew that some oth
strength was bearing her along.

"I may lose him," she thought; "he w
go away; I must make him go away-
until——"

She struggled here like one breathlessly mbing the last steep slope of some ight.

"Yes; he must go. Perhaps he will aderstand. But will he ever come back me?"

She knelt and prayed that Lutterel's ve might last.

CHAPTER X

THE doctor came. He examined Parslo
and then asked to speak with Elsie i
the room below. He looked at the dea
whiteness of her suffering face and at th
shadows under her eyes.

"Signora——"

She wondered what he was going to sa
to her.

"He is better?"

"I think he will live."

She folded cold, spirit hands over th
burning love within. She looked at hin
with eyes of tragedy.

"How long?" she asked.

He half turned away; he was aware o
the tragic cry behind that question.

"I can't say. A month, a year, te
years. It may depend on—you, signora."

"On me!"

Her hands were pressed to her bosom.

"Yes; he must live very quietly, with
out emotion, without excitement. Gently
No worries; no shocks."

She stood very still. Her eyes had a lind look as though her vision was turned ıward upon a world of renunciation, nguish, patience, and suspense.

"I will do my best" she said.

She felt that she was closing a door, ıe door of her own heart.

When the doctor had gone she went ut into the garden, knowing that she ould find Lutterel there waiting to hear is fate. The morning was fragrant, and as ıe passed through all the half wild beauty f the garden she prayed that he would e gentle with her and that he would not lead passionately with her to surrender verything and go away with him. She elt that she could not bear the pain of ithstanding him, perhaps of seeing him eave her with impatience and in anger.

She saw the boat lying on the shingle, ut Lutterel was not to be seen. She alled, softly, like a sad bird calling its ıate.

"Geoff—Geoff, where are you?"

His voice answered from the cypresses bove.

"Here. Shall I come to you?"

"Wait there," she said.

She found him walking up and dow
between the rows of cypresses, and whe
he saw her rising out of the undergrowt
which masked the path, he came slowl
towards her like a man walking in a churcl
He was master of himself; she knew that a
once. His eyes looked at her with a tende
ness which hovered but did not touch. Hi
love had the greatness of a sensitive re
straint, and when she realized it she wa
grateful.

"Elsie, you have had no sleep."

She gave him the ghost of a smile.

"And you?"

"I have been thinking hard," he said.

His eyes waited on her, and with a ligh
touch of the fingers he guided her to th
little white temple. They sat down her
on the semi-circular stone seat, and th
white pillars cut the blue of sea and sky
There was a humming of insects every
where, and among the olives on the hi
behind them a man was singing.

Lutterel held her hand.

"Tell me," he said.

"The doctor thinks he will live. He wi
be helpless; everything will depend on me."

"Elsie!"

She held his hand firmly.

"Geoff, help me. I cannot leave him
ow. He is what he is—but could I
eave him there—helpless—and go away?
hould we be happy? Should I be happy?
Iy dear, I love you, and yet I cannot go."

He sat very still. His arm crept up
ntil his open hand clasped her head, and
rawing it gently, made it rest against
is head. They remained thus, cheek
gainst cheek.

"Elsie—what makes you feel like this?"

"I don't know," she said; "I don't
now. Perhaps it is because I love you
o much, and my love will not let me do a
hing which I could never forget. Do you
nderstand?"

"Yes," he said; "I think I understand."

He turned his face and softly kissed her
air.

"Dear, it is because I love you as I do
hat I understand; and, though it hurts
ne, I love you for your fineness, your
enerosity."

"Oh, Geoff," she said, "I'm not fine—
eally. Something drives me."

"A second martyrdom," he said sadly,
'a second martyrdom. Perhaps it is

because I am a bit of a woman that understand."

They remained for a while in silence cheek to cheek.

"Elsie," he said presently, "I shal wait."

He felt a slight tremor pass through her

"Geoff, it won't be fair to you. Tim changes things. And, oh—my dear—couldn't bear——"

"What couldn't you bear?" he asked.

"To live here on a promise, feeling tha you were tied. Don't promise me anything."

Again he kissed her hair and with man's reverence.

"Very well; I'll make you no spoken promise, Elsie, but I want you to mak me one."

"What is it, Geoff?"

"That you will write to me—when—when you are free. Just three words 'It is over.' Promise me this."

"I promise," she said.

CHAPTER XI

Six months passed, and Jacob Parsloe remained a wreck. He had regained the partial use of one arm and leg, but he was unable to walk or to lift himself out of bed or out of a chair, and he had to be dressed, washed and fed. In the old days he had been accustomed to boast of his vocabulary, and he had been left with three words—"Elsie"—"Sorry"—and "Atomical," a queer three-belled peal upon which he had to ring the changes. He understood all that was said to him, and in time Elsie grew extraordinarily quick in divining his wants and in supplying them.

She nursed him with great conscientiousness and some kindness, and he was unhappy when she was out of his sight.

But Parsloe the paralytic was different from Parsloe the philosopher. The change was there, and Elsie felt it, and in his way he would manage to make her feel it. His eyes expressed a sort of surprised gentleness.

Her way of communicating with him was the method of trial by error. When he wished to tell her something he would utter her name—"Elsie," and repeat it several times, and she would begin her catechism. "You want the shutters closed. You want me to read to you. You would like a drink. Your pillows aren't comfortable. You want me to go for a walk, for a drive." His "sorry" meant yes, his "atomical" no. But what she began to discover was that he was thinking far more of her and less of himself. Often and often his thoughts concerned her pleasure or her comfort, and she was hard put to it to find out what he wanted her to do.

"Am I to go to Santa Maria?"

"Sorry, sorry."

"Am I to buy something?"

"Sorry."

"For you?"

"Atomical, atomical."

"For myself?"

"Sorry, sorry."

"A dress? Anything that pleases me?"

"Sorry, sorry."

She was touched. She realized that the helpless mass of tissue held another sort of man from the man who had been her husband. In his helpless, stammering way he wanted to make things up to her.

Yet, she did not realize how strong this feeling was until he made her understand that he wished his English lawyer to come out to Italy. She had to write a letter for him, and the lawyer came.

She was not present at the interview between them, for Parsloe had intimated that he wished her to be absent. She had prompted the solicitor as to the method of procedure, warning him that he would have to go on asking questions until he asked the right ones and got the required answers. He understood.

And Parsloe made his will.

"I shall not live long. I want to leave everything to my wife."

"Unconditionally?"

"Sorry," said the man on the bed.

CHAPTER XII

Anna—not the sullen Anna of old—had said to her that morning: "The signora looks beautiful in black." Her mirror repeated all that Anna said, making much of her bronze head and the cream of her skin in contrast to that simple sheath of black.

She looked at herself in the mirror with an air of questioning aloofness.

"That is you, Elsie—a widow! Does it matter how you look?"

A week ago she had written that letter, "It is over"; just that brief message and no more, and for seven silent days she had waited, and no message had come to her in return.

Had he forgotten? Had he ceased to care? She wondered; always, she had made herself ask this question, braving it as she had learnt to brave other things which a woman must face. She was glad that she had refused to let him make her a promise, sorrowfully glad, but now she knew that she wanted him as she had never wanted him before. A year's sacrifice was at an end. It had left her empty, lonely, with nothing to do.

Would he come?

She protested that she did not know.

That eighth morning she spent in the garden, wandering along the familiar paths, and renewing the many memories that the garden held for her. She sat on the stone seat in the little white temple; she descended the path to the rocky inlet where she had helped to save Lutterel from the sea.

"It all happened a year ago," said a voice within. "Does he remember it as I do remember it?"

She passed the afternoon sitting in one of the great, cool rooms with the shutters closed, and a book on her knee, but she did not read. She was too conscious of time, of the hours which carried her with them as they flowed away towards some unknown night or dawn. Her heart beat out the day like a clock, another day, a voiceless day, empty of all happening. She was calm; she clung to this calmness, she even wrapped it about her like a nun's garment, telling herself that she might need it and nothing else.

After tea she walked again in the garden, making of it a cloister in which her thoughts were unvexed by doubts and yearnings. She refused to let herself look towards the coast road from Santa Maria, that dusty white thread winding in and out at the foot of the cliffs. She would not let herself question the silence of that outer world, or wonder whether its silence had the finality of death.

Towards evening she returned to the house. She opened the shutters and sat down by her window. She could see the rocks, and the quiet sea with the sunlight touching it, but the sun was near the hills, and another day was dying.

"He has forgotten," she thought. "He does not wish to remember."

And then, suddenly, she sat erect, pale, listening. She had heard the sound of a bell, the bell at the gate, and the clatter of Anna's footsteps as she crossed the hall and went down into the garden.

An age seemed to pass; she felt faint, dizzy.

Then, she heard his voice in the hall, the voice of her lover.

THE HOUSE BEHIND THE JUDAS TREE

By GILBERT FRANKAU

THE HOUSE BEHIND THE JUDAS TREE

CHAPTER I

I HAD been taking pleasure in a new aspect of known beauty—pines a-climb up the Esterels, vineyards, grey-green olives, a triangle of blue Mediterranean pinched between red cliff-fangs—when my engine faltered, coughed, and gave up its job.

"Serves me right for giving my chauffeur the afternoon off," said I, and got down to inspect the trouble.

Five minutes showed the trouble beyond my amateur repairing. Only a fool or an expert tinkers with his magneto. So, having cursed mine, I lit a cigarette and considered my position.

The Route Nationale lay ten kilomètres behind and below me. Right and left were only rocks and pine saplings. Ahead, towards the empty sea-coast, over the slope between the golden broom-hedges, a pale-blue wisp of smoke petered out in the gold glimmer of the sky.

I made for the smoke-wisp, and came, topping the contour, on a lonely house. A Judas tree just in bloom sheltered that house, and through the pale puce of the laden branches I was aware of white pigeons a-strut on red tiles, and of yellow roses climbing a little porch that was all Provence. Between me and the porch ran a breast-high wall, and over the iron gate in that wall leaned a man in a grey linen shirt, wide open of collar, with his head bare to the sun.

The head was handsome, if a trifle forbidding; the hair of it jet-black and curly; the eyes very dark and sunk deep in big sockets under a straight penthouse of thick brow.

"*Pardonnez-moi, monsieur*——" began I, and told my tale.

Talking, I was aware of no friendliness. My man, with his fiercely-upcurled black moustachios, his stocky figure, his cleft chin, and his sun-browned complexion, might have been a gendarme listening to a complaint of burglary, or a French country lawyer weighing the evidence of a crime.

But when I had done speaking, very red lips disclosed the whitest of square teeth, and a voice with a melodious roll, yet a certain diffidence, answered:

"No doubt we can do something for you, sir; but, meanwhile, will you not come in?"

The gate was opened for me, and I went in under the puce canopy of the Judas tree, down a flagged path between the yellow roses, into the shade of the porch.

"Wait here," said my man—and left me, shouting: "Rafael! Rafael! Where are you? Come quickly. Come at once!"

A voice from somewhere behind the house answered:

"I am here, monsieur."

And almost immediately my man was back, followed by another, obviously a servant, a queer-looking fellow, little, but with the shoulders of a Hercules and a prizefighter's hands.

Prizefighter, perhaps, is the aptest description of Rafael. He had the big, broken nose of one, and the flattened cheekbones, and the mop of inky hair. He was clean-shaven, too, and bare-armed in a thin singlet. But his brown eyes were more of the dog than the human, and while he listened to his master's repetition of my story they kept turning to me—not exactly in suspicion, but with doubt.

When the story was finished, master and servant held a consultation over it.

"What is to be done, Rafael?"

"There is my bicycle, monsieur. I could ride to Fréjus. The garagist could send a mechanic——"

"But would he?"

"I think so, monsieur. If one explained to him——"

"And dinner?"

"Ah, I had forgotten dinner!"

"Dinner would be very late, Rafael."

"Too late for monsieur. Perhaps a car will pass. I could signal it——"

"But would it stop, think you?"

"That depends, monsieur. Of a certainty, the garagist would be better. Only monsieur must eat."

"And this gentleman, too, must eat. You see, it is already after seven."

"Does monsieur, indeed, suggest——"

"But why not, Rafael?"

"There is enough, of course."

"Why not, then?"

"That is not for me to say. That is as monsieur wishes."

A slight pause followed, and during it I, feeling a little uncomfortable, made up my mind to seek other help.

"Please do not trouble——" I began, only to be interrupted by a determined:

"But it is no trouble, monsieur. It will be a pleasure if only you will dine with me. Honestly, it will be a pleasure. And afterwards, Rafael here shall ride his bicycle into Fréjus, as he suggests."

So the three of us—though Rafael could have accomplished it single-handed—went along the road and pushed my light car as far as the Judas tree, and left it there and went back to the house.

One is not a story-teller for nothing, and in the half-hour that followed I found it difficult to keep my curiosity in check. My host, contrary to foreign custom, did not introduce himself. He asked no personal questions, and vouchsafed no personal information.

CHAPTER II

OVER our *apéritif* which Rafael, still eyeing me like a dog in doubt of my intentions, brought to the porch on a tray of spotless silver, he seemed at a loss for speech. The Dubonnet drunk, he showed me round his garden, a gem of its kind.

"You must keep a considerable staff?" I suggested, regarding the many flowers, the trim rows of vegetables, the fruit-trees, the chicken-run, the clean rabbit-house with its porcelain water-trough and its nets for the green leaves.

"I have only Rafael," said he.

I looked at his hands then. But the well-kept finger-nails and the soft, slightly hairy skin were not those of the gardener; and once we had finished our inspection of the garden and went into the long Provençal living-room, my curiosity at finding such a man and such a house in the loneliest part of the Esterels was almost more than the story-teller in me could bear.

For the room, like the garden, was a gem. The sun, slanting now through the square, deeply-embrasured windows, showed me treasures of walnut furniture, of Aubusson carpets of carved ivory and fretted silver. And all the pieces of silver shone as the tray from which Rafael had handed us our *apéritifs;* and the furniture shone with them; and the parquet might have been highly-polished glass.

At the very end of the room, over a stone chimney-piece that museum-keepers might have envied, hung a picture, obviously modern, but in a fine old frame. And because the picture was that of a woman, young and dark and very lovely, my copy-hunter's mind leaped to the easiest solution of the mystery I had begun to scent.

"A man and his mistress," I thought. "Isolating themselves. Because of a scandal, perhaps."

But my host, seeing the direction my eyes had taken, said—speaking, I thought, with some constraint on him:

"My poor wife, monsieur. She is dead."

"A recluse," I decided then. "Passion lorn." Yet though I guessed him passionate above the average, the explanation failed to satisfy me. Because why should a country garage-proprietor refuse help to a mere recluse—and why, if a mere recluse's servant signalled it, should a passing car refuse to stop?

"She must have been very beautiful," I went on, approaching the picture.

"She was all that, monsieur."

My host said no more—only stood there, very still, while I examined the ripe brush-work which portrayed, as no words can, a face of dreams. There were a thousand moods in that face, and a thousand riddles, and a thousand separate exquisitenesses. Losing it, a man might well feel that he had lost his all.

Yet even so, a man, obviously not poor, need not live, apparently with no other means of transport than his servant's bicycle, in this outlandish place.

It was the servant—I imagined a little later—even more than the master, who really mystified me. For when, after I had washed in a tiled cloak-room, he came to announce the dinner, he had completely metamorphosed himself—from the bare-armed, mop-headed prizefighter into the almost perfect *maître-d'hôtel.*

"The gentlemen are served," he announced, standing stiffly in his cut-away coat and dark trousers—and soon we were being served, in that same shining living-room, with a dinner that would not have put Brillat Savarin himself to shame.

* * *

Our menu was of the simplest. But it had been prepared, as it was served, by an artist—and during it we spoke but little, because a super-artist had chosen the dry, amber-coloured wine.

Coffee followed, steaming hot from silver Paul Lamerie spout to cups of genuine blue Sèvres china; and the unlabelled brandy, my palate told me, could not have been young in '65. But when, drawing courage from cognac, I ventured to my benefactor, "Can it be that such a *chef* as yours, sir, actually helps in your house and garden?" I was answered, "I have no *chef.* There is only Rafael. In this house, as I told you, there is only Rafael and I."

"Then the age of miracles is not passed," I retorted, thinking of my own rustic servants; and he, for his tongue, too, had been a little loosened, "perhaps you are right, sir. Perhaps it is a miracle when a man finds gratitude in this ungrateful post-War world."

Despite all the mental restfulness inspired by such a dinner, the word "post-War" set my curiosity, and my imagination, working again. Had these two been through the war-fire together? Was that their bond?

For obviously—other mysteries apart—there must be a bond. Since no man would render, for mere wages, that perfect service which this Rafael was rendering to my host.

And besides, it wasn't only the actual service. It was the devotion—that simple dog-like devotion which I had noticed there at the very outset, and which had kept on displaying itself all through dinner in Rafael's eyes.

"Yes," I went on; "gratitude is a rare quality these days. Especially in the servant-classes."

"And in women," said my host.

Then he bit his lip, as one who has been betrayed into a confidence, and fell silent, a queer look in his eyes.

I respected his silence; and we must have sat there, under the picture of his dead wife, for a good five minutes; till Rafael came in, soft-footed, and removed the coffee-cups.

"If monsieur does not require me further," said Rafael, "I will take my *velo* and ride to Fréjus."

"You have eaten, then?"

"*Oui, monsieur.*"

"Very well."

CHAPTER III

TWILIGHT was falling, almost as swiftly as it falls in the tropics, when my nameless host and I left the dinner-table. The outlines of the big Provençal living-room were a little blurred; and the face of the picture which had looked down on us all the while we were dining grew indistinct, shadowy. I remember that I turned to take a last look at that face, seeing it only as a pale oval in a dark setting, before we passed out into the porch.

The two chairs in the porch had been rearranged, and a table set between them. On the table were more glasses, a cut crystal decanter, a bottle of mineral water, a lighted lamp. Moths fluttered round the lamp, and the scent of the yellow roses was heady in the gathering darkness. As we sat down I saw Rafael—again in his prize-fighter garb—wheel his bicycle to the gate.

"He can scarcely be back within the hour," said my host. And then, with the first flicker of personal interest: "Do you live far from here?"

"About fifty kilomètres."

"At Cannes, perhaps?"

"No. On the Côte des Maures."

"Ah!" A pause. "You are a foreigner, of course?"

"Yes, I am English."

"A great country, England. If a little inhuman."

"Inhuman, sir?"

"But, yes. Were this England, I should not have my Rafael. And without my Rafael——"

He broke off, biting his lips again. But I could see that the racial need for speech was on him; and presently, across the lamplight, the dark eyes in the big sockets looked anxiously into mine.

"Not only racial," I thought then. "His need goes deeper."

And just as I was thinking that, he began talking, rather quickly, his words toppling over one another—as words will topple over one another after long disuse.

"Perhaps I owe you no explanation," he began. "Perhaps you are not even interested. Yet, somehow, I think you are interested in—in this house and this Rafael of mine, who is—though perhaps I should not say so—the perfect valet, the perfect *chef*, the perfect housemaid, and the perfect gardener combined. To you—you said as much—he seems a miracle. But to me—as I told you—the miracle is the gratitude. And that the gratitude should go on."

A big moth, one wing scorched in the lamp-flame, interrupted by falling on the table; and my host, having killed it with a flick of the finger and a stamp of shoe-sole, suggested that we drink. I noticed that his hand shook a little as he unstoppered the decanter; and that his eyes avoided mine.

* * *

"My poor wife and I were just married when Rafael first came to us," he went on. "Shortly after the War, that was. I did not live here then. I lived a little way out of Cannes, on the road to Grasse. A big house we had, and a fine garden, and several servants, and a car. Rafael was the lowest of our servants—the garden-man, the boot-cleaner, the coal-breaker, the filler of the furnace. We saw him seldom. Yet whenever we did see him he always smiled. One day I asked him why he always smiled; and he said, 'Because I am happy in monsieur's service. Because I am saving money. And because, when I have saved enough money, I shall be able to make a fine marriage—like monsieur.'

"A simple soul, you will observe. With our common French ambition—to work, to save, to mate. 'But when you marry,' I told him, 'you will want to leave us.' '*Mais pourquoi?*' he answered. 'Could not my wife, too, serve monsieur and madame?' And then, one evening, he introduced to us the girl who was to become his wife."

My host hesitated on that last sentence; and, watching him, I saw his hand shake again, ever so slightly, as he lifted the glass to his lips.

"In those days," he went on, "I was not, as I am now, a *rentier*. I had a business—a law business—in Cannes. Every morning my chauffeur would drive me to my office. In the evening he would fetch me. Usually my wife would come with him. It was on one such evening, I remember, that I first saw Fernande. She was waiting for us, with Rafael, when we came back to the villa. And I—I distrusted her from the first. She was sly, I thought; and ferrety—with her lath of a figure, and her pale hair, and her pale eyebrows, and her little claw-like hands. She was slightly hunchbacked too; and her way of speaking irritated me. She minced her words. 'A shop-girl,' I decided, while Rafael was introducing her to us. And as it happened, I was right.

"Rafael, of course, was very proud of being *fiancé* with a shop-girl. For him it would be a splendid marriage. Only Fernande was not so very strong—not quite strong enough for the shop, anyway. So perhaps if madame wanted someone to look after her clothes, her lingerie——'But we have no room for another *ménage*,' my wife told them. 'And besides, you are not married yet, Rafael. Perhaps you never will be married. Supposing Fernande here should change her mind?'

"The girl laughed at that, and said something I did not gather. But Rafael looked—how shall I put it?—like a savage dog when one threatens to take away his bone.

I saw his teeth bared and his eyes go sullen, and one of his big hands working. And I knew then—I told my wife as much after they had left us—just the kind of hold Fernande had on him. My poor wife, I remember, said: 'So much the better for her, then. For he is a low type, our Rafael. There would be no other way to hold him. But she, one feels, has intelligence.' 'Not intelligence,' said I. 'Cunning.' For as I told you, I distrusted the woman from the first."

CHAPTER IV

BECAUSE, perhaps, of that racial difference which makes your Englishman, who is generally over-diffuse with his pen, a terse talker, and your Frenchmen, so terse in his literature, over-voluble in speech, it seems better that I should give only a few impressions I gathered during the next part of my host's tale.

Those impressions, doubtless, have been a little coloured by subsequent knowledge. Yet even at the time they were unfavourable to him—because of the hatred in his voice.

I have heard stark hatred in a man's voice before; but never that peculiar virulence which grated on me every time my Frenchman spoke the name, "Fernande."

"A bad type," he kept on saying. "She had the devil in her. She had the *mauvais caractère*. But my poor wife did not realize it. When Rafael married, she insisted he must bring her into the house."

The girl, Fernande, I gathered, came into my host's establishment as sewing-maid—and apparently she did her work well. Her mistress seemed to have taken a fancy to her, to have found her companionable. "Sometimes, my poor wife would take her shopping; and she would be sitting with the chauffeur when the car fetched me from the office. Out-of-doors, she dressed too well for a servant. And she used to scent herself like—like a cheap *cocotte*."

I imagined, though he never said as much, that my Frenchman and his young wife must have had their first quarrels about Fernande; he certainly tried, more then once, in the first six months of Rafael's marriage, to get the girl out of his house. But by the end of those six months, she must have consolidated her position with her mistress. And by that time Rafael had made himself too useful to sack.

The impression he tried to give me of Rafael, during this period, was supremely pathetic. "He adored her, you see; and she was sly enough, cunning enough, to make him do two men's work for her. And when our other *mênage* left us, three."

According to my host, his "other *ménage*," a chambermaid and a house-parlourmaid, who had been with him when he was a bachelor, did not leave willingly. His wife, under the influence of Fernande, dismissed them—promoting Fernande and Rafael in their place. "Oh, but she was artful, I tell you. She must have told some tale about them. I ought to have protested. But *que voulez-vous*, a household is a wife's job, not a husband's. And besides, it meant an economy. We got the chauffeur to help with the boots and the furnace. Till he, too, left."

That also—the loss of his old chauffeur—my Frenchman attributed to the wife of Rafael. Yet he seemed to have made no protest when that "miserable woman" suggested that a cousin of hers, one Robert, should take the vacant place. "*Que voulez-vous?* Servants were scarce, and the man had got good references. And my poor wife could not drive herself. She was too nervous, too highly-strung."

Fernande's cousin, however, after his first week or so, refused to have anything to do with the boots or the furnace-filling.

So Rafael, in the words of the poet, "took on that duty as well."

Except for a woman cook, somewhat hard of hearing and a little short-sighted, the villa on the Grasse road must, by this time, have been almost as much of a "one-man show" as the Provençal house in which I heard the tale of it. "Fernande certainly looked after my wife's clothes; but otherwise she did nothing. Nothing whatever I tell you. She made her husband work for her, for all of us. And he was so good. He never grumbled. No hours were too long for him, no task too difficult. Because he adored her; because he adored that little horror of a Fernande."

CHAPTER V

HATRED, possibly, is catching. Be that as it may, however, it was just after he had used his expression, "that little horror of a Fernande," that I first experienced an actual dislike of my nameless host. Something, I felt, was wrong about the man; and something abnormal; and something —how shall I put it?—false.

"Why," I asked myself, "is he telling me all this rigmarole? It explains nothing —except, perhaps, Rafael's competence as a servant."

Yet, for all my growing dislike of the man (there came a moment, later on, when I could hardly bear to look at him) he interested me. And, in a way, though he used too many of them, he was an artist in words.

His words, as they continued, drew me a picture—or rather a series of pictures. I saw the villa on the Grasse road—formal and rather elaborate, with its tiled mansarde for the indoor servants, and its green shutters overlooking a gravelled courtyard, and its garden of palms and pine-trees, its lodge where the chauffeur slept, and the garage for the car.

The chauffeur, Robert, I saw, too—as a little mouse-coloured fellow, rather like his cousin; good at his job, but secretive; and thinking himself, as his cousin thought herself, a very superior being to Rafael, who bore with him as he bore with the deaf cook, who seemed to have been somewhat of a tyrant—the sort who refuses to clean her own dishes, and goes to bed early, leaving someone else to do the washing-up.

But of my host, and especially of his dead wife, I got only glimpses—through Fernande.

Fernande, as he told it, was the protagonist of my host's story; an evil presence, pervading all their lives. To him she was always the sly, obedient servant: but to the rest of the household, a termagant, with the unreasonableness of a mental defective and the temper of a fiend. She and the cook were hardly on speaking terms. Her husband she treated like a dog; demanding even, on occasions, a separate room from him. To her cousin, though she would sometimes condescend to flirt with him, she was haughtily contemptous. With her mistress, she permitted herself "liberties"—though how far such liberties went I was not informed.

About this time, too—some two years after her marriage—Fernande refused to wear servant's clothes any more, and went about what household duties she could not contrive to put on her husband looking "more like a cheap *cocotte* than ever"—and with an insolence you would not believe.

"Half a dozen times," said my nameless host, "I would have remonstrated with her; but always my poor wife pleaded with me." And after that, the overflow of his words dimished and he began to speak very softly, more to himself than to me.

"Women," he went on, in that new soft voice. "They are all alike, really. When once they take a certain path, one can do nothing with them. So Rafael and—so my poor Rafael was quite powerless. Though by that time I think he had begun to understand—not all, of course, but omething of the way this woman was :ating him up.

"All women are vampires, really. But .his Fernande, she was worse than most)f them. She ate him up, I tell you. For :very morsel she gave of herself she took ıer pound of flesh from him. The strength)f his body she took, and the joy of his ;oul. Once he had been all smiles. Now ıe never smiled at me. His face was sullen because of the overwork she put on him. And because of her lies.

"It was about me she would lie to him—saying how mean I was, grudging them their little holidays and their wine. 'Madame,' she used to say, 'was an angel. With her alone they might have been quite happy. But never with monsieur.'

"How did I know that? I didn't. Not until long afterwards. Yet I knew enough to understand that her influence worked against me, and that she was turning my house into a misery. And one day I spoke to my poor wife about it. 'In the name of Heaven,' I said, 'let us get rid of these two. Let us be happy together, as we used to be before this creature came into our lives.' But my poor wife would not listen. 'If Fernande and Rafael go,' she said, 'Robert will go with them. And I feel so safe with Robert. He drives so carefully.' So in the end though it was difficult for me, I spoke to Rafael. Not as his master, you will understand, but as his friend. 'You do too much,' I told him. 'Your wife should help you more. And you should control your wife. You should stand less nonsense from her.' He took it badly, that first time—because of the lies she had told him about me. But later—later he came to see that I was in the right.

"We were both right, of course. Yet even after I had brought him to my opinion, Rafael, though he tried, could do nothing with her. She had that hold on him, you see. The sex-hold. *L'amour*. Because of it he could not even beat her, as all who have the *mauvais caractère* should be beaten, with a whip.

"Yes, with a whip. You shudder when I say that. Being English, you do not believe in the whipping of women. Yet in your law you English are more inhuman than we are. In your law you

make no allowance for the emotions. Your
law is cold. Cold."

That was the moment—and I have no
hesitation in confessing it—when I could
hardly bear to look at my Frenchman;
when the very glint in his eyes, the very
tone of his voice, nauseated me; when I
began to long very desperately for Rafael's
return with the garagist.

But the road beyond the Judas tree
carried no sound either of car-horn or
cycle-bell, and in another moment the
copy-hunter's curiosity conquered nausea,
and I set myself to listen again, so intently
that, even as I sit here writing, memory
brings back each and every word.

CHAPTER VI

"YOUR law" runs the word. "What does it know of men such as—such as Rafael? The man of passion is like a wolf. He mates once and once only But the wolf has the better of it becaus his mate is loyal. He was loyal enough my Rafael. Loyal and very foolish, an very blind. Maybe we are all a littl blind when *l'amour* is on us. I have ofter thought so since—since I became a widower. But the blindness of Rafael wa worse than—than most people's. And h was chivalrous. Yes, chivalrous—I ca give it no other name.

"He could have thrashed her so easily you see. And she, Fernande, was that kind. She would have taken it from him Her, even the threat of it might have cured—— But he would not. 'She is not strong,' he used to say. 'Monsieu does not understand how little strong sh is. But monsieur's comfort shall not suffer.

His work shall be done for him. Because I—I am stronger than ten horses.' For to me also—once we understood one another—the man was loyal.

"He was loyal to everyone. Yes, to every single one of us. Even to Robert, her cousin, though in the end Robert would sneer at him openly. '*Que voulez-vous, monsieur?*' he used to tell me, when I upbraided him for tolerating these sneers. 'Robert is of the family, and so long as he serves monsieur and madame faithfully——' But I—I had learned to distrust Robert, even more than I distrusted Fernande. Of an afternoon, when he used to take her and my poor wife driving, I would be nervous. If the three of them were late in fetching me from the office—and they were often late—I would be almost frantic. And she, Fernande, always knew the state I was in. She used to grin at me, like a monkey, from her seat on the box.

"Robert never grinned. *His* face would be expressionless. Yet about him, too, there was that something sly, ferrety. Only he, that one, had intelligence as well as cunning. So that it was only by accident I found out. And when I did find out—— But listen! Let me tell you the thing just as it occurred.

"We, my poor wife and I, had been married four years by that time; Rafael and his Fernande, three. It was a busy moment on the Côte d'Azur. The land-boom had begun, and I was making much money, working very late. Sometimes I could not get home till seven, sometimes till after nine. For that reason I gave up bothering my head about the household. As long as Robert was at the door by eight-thirty in the morning, as long as supper was on the table when I came back to the villa, it sufficed.

"Even about my poor wife, in those days, I could bother very little. What would you? When one is trying to make a fortune one may be allowed to neglect a woman. And she—she never remonstrated. '*Pauvre chéri,*' she used to say. 'So weary!' And on the nights when I was weariest, she made me sleep alone.

"Usually, I slept without waking—though it seemed strange, after those four years, not to have her beside me. Once or twice, however, I imagined that my sleep had been broken by the noise of a motor-engine. Also, I used to dream of lights sweeping above my head. And then, on one particular night, I found that I was not dreaming, that the lights were real. But I only saw them circle across the ceiling; and before I could get the shutters open they were gone.

"'Some passing car,' I thought, as I climbed into bed again. But next day, thinking the affair over, I realized that no passing car-lights could possibly throw their beams from the road through the screen of wall and high trees to my window; and that if the lights had indeed been car-lights they must have come to my own garage, through my own gate.

* * *

"'So that's the game, is it?' I thought—for, as I told you, I mistrusted the man; and two evenings later I made an excuse to sit in front with Master Robert when he drove me home from the office. And next morning, when he drove me back to the office, I sat in front again.

"I had not slept alone that night. And my wife's room faced away from the garage. So neither his lights nor the noise of his engine had disturbed me. But overnight, the speedometer-reading had advanced by fifty kilometres. And on the next evening I—I laid my trap

"I was a lawyer then. So I did not lay my trap clumsily. And because I was a lawyer, I felt that I ought to have at least one witness. But which one? My poor wife, of course, must be kept out of it. The cook? But she was very deaf and a little short-sighted. Some outsider perhaps? But it was hardly an affair for an outsider. In the end, therefore, I decided to make Rafael when—when once I had watched my fox out of the lodge-gates, and locked them behind him so that he could not get back.

"Those gates I locked a little after midnight, when the rest of the household were sleeping; and I confess that I could not help chuckling a little as I watched Master Robert's red rear-light disappear at a good eighty for Cannes. 'When you come back, my fine fellow,' I said to myself, 'you won't feel quite so happy.' Then I went back to my room, and read for an hour. And at about half-past one I went upstairs into the mansarde, and tapped, not too loudly, on Rafael's door.

"He did not wake at once. He was too tired, poor fellow. But at last I managed to arouse him, and he called out to me, '*Qu'est que c'est? Qui est là?*'

"'*C'est moi,*' I called back. 'Your master. Come quickly.'

"He came almost at once, tangle-haired sleepy-eyed, his trousers over his night-shirt. When he reached the door, I asked about Fernande—whether she still slept.

"'Fernande sleeps in the other room to-night, monsieur,' he told me. 'She had one of her headaches. Does monsieur wish that I should waken her? Is there a doctor to be sent for? Does monsieur require Robert? Is monsieur or madame perhaps, ill?'

"'Nobody is ill,' I said. 'And Fernande must not be woken. But I need you. Follow me, and be silent. So he followed me, in his slippers, down the stairs.

*   *   *

"I had wondered whether, when he knew what I required of him, he would be reluctant. Robert was his cousin by marriage, you see. And at first he was a little reluctant. But after—after I had worked on him a little, he consented to do what I asked.

"'All I want *you* to do,' I said, 'is to be a witness. If you are with me, and Robert has some explanation of his conduct, so much the better for him.' So presently we slipped out into the garden and waited by the lodge-gates for my fox to come back.

"He kept us waiting longer than I had expected; but at last we heard his engine. 'When he alights to try to open the gates,' I said, 'but not before that, I shall go forward. You will come with me—and hear what I have to say.'

"'It shall be as monsieur wishes,' he answered; and just after that we saw the first glare of the lights. But the lights advanced only slowly; and perhaps they dazzled me more than they dazzled Rafael. Because even when the beams of them came abreast of us, even when the car stopped, I did not see what Rafael saw. I only waited, as I said I would wait, for Robert to get down from his box. And even when Robert did not get down immediately, I suspected nothing—nothing whatever, I tell you—till Rafael rushed past me, till I saw him leap for and clamber up the gateway, till I heard his fists thud, and the first choke from Robert, his cousin, and Fernande's scream.

"She screamed all the while he was choking the life out of Robert. And I tried to get to her. But, before I had managed to unlock the lodge-gates, it was too late."

CHAPTER VII

"It was too late."

The words petered out there; and my man, his need for speech gone, hunched sullen in the lamp-light. Another moth immolated itself; but he made no attempt to put the winged thing out of its agony. And watching him thus, I shuddered again. For, as I have said, one is not a story-teller for nothing; and all through the last part of his tale my sense of criticism had been at work, telling me how false the thing rang, and how many gaps there were in it. And as imagination tried to fill those gaps, I thought:

"You hated that Fernande from the first. And your hatred grew on you. You set her husband against her. You worked on him, till you almost made him use the whip on her. You told him she was a liar. What else did you tell him? Did you, by any chance, know when you laid your trap 'not clumsily' for Robert—that Fernande, too, would be found in it? But why did you lay that trap? And why did you mistrust Robert? And why are you telling me, a complete stranger, all this?"

Also—and this is strange—I had a distinct vision of the man, not hunched in the lamp-light, but standing—standing still—standing quite still in semi-darkness. And in my vision I heard no screams—only the deep, bitter sobbing of that other man who had killed twice for love's sake, as he knelt over a still-warm body where stationary car-lights shimmered down a long, empty road.

On our road, too—on the hill-road beyond the Judas tree—all was silent. But presently, after I had put the winged thing between us out of its agony, I heard the far honk of a motor-car and the clack of a bad gear-gauge as it took the slope.

"He was acquitted?" I asked quickly.

"But, of course"—he, too, spoke quickly —"Rafael had no intent to murder them. In our law, which is not inhuman, there must be pre-intent to murder. And, besides, when he saw her in her lover's arms, when he saw them kissing one another, his emotions——"

"Was that corroborated?"

"The kiss, you mean?"

"Yes."

"The jury took his word for it, monsieur."

"Yet it must have been your evidence or——"

"Not only my evidence. But my money, my skill, my knowledge. That is why he is so grateful. That is why, when I became a widower, when I decided to give up my law business, he came with me. That is why he has learned to make life so comfortable for me. That is why——"

The car on the road honked, changed gear again. Its light flashed on us. Then it stopped; and my host's voice, which had grown suddenly unsteady, stopped with it; and in another second Rafael stood before us, smiling a little, as one who has done a difficult task well.

"He is outside, monsieur," said Rafael to his master; and to me: "If you will go to him, if you will explain what is the matter."

I went out alone, neither of them volunteering to accompany me; and found, to my surprise, that a thick-set surly fellow in stained blue overalls was already roping my dumb-irons to his own luggage grid.

"But perhaps you can repair her here," I suggested.

"Not here, monsieur," he grunted; "at the garage, perhaps."

So I left him to his roping, and went back to thank my host for my dinner, and to tip Rafael for his help.

I complimented Rafael on his cooking, of course; and with his master, as is the habit of the country, I shook hands.

The hand was smaller than my own, smooth and queerly attractive. Yet it felt clammy; and in it I sensed tension. It seemed to me that it wanted to rid itself of my presence.

"Don't come back," it seemed to be impressing on me. And *I* thought, all my dislike suddenly renewing itself, "Don't worry. I'll never come back to you. I'll never visit this house again."

* * *

Yet I know now that I would have visited that house again—because the garagist, as I have indicated, was the sort of fellow who kept his own counsel, and because a mystery is a mystery, however strong a dislike one may have taken to the guardian of it, had it not been for my chauffeur's wife, whom I found waiting up for me with her husband, and who said, her face paling, when I told them how I had got my dinner:

"But, *bon dieu*, monsieur! Monsieur has dined in the house which nobody visits—in the house of the Two Homicides."

"Two!" said I, sleepily, for it had been a long tow from Fréjus.

"*Mais oui, monsieur*. They are both homicides. Maître Gouraud, he shot his rich foreign wife, monsieur. About two years ago it was. Pim pom. Just like that, he shot her—even though she had the *grosse fortune*—one afternoon when she came to fetch him from his office. She had a lover, you see; one she used to spend the afternoons with. Maître Gouraud had suspected her for a long time. But he could find out nothing, because of a faithful maid and a faithful chauffeur she had. It was only after they were out of the way, killed by that other one——"

But who is the real killer? The wolf—or the man who looses the wolf for his own sordid purposes? And, if you remember, as I remembered, lying sleepless, how Fernande used to grin at this Maître Gouraud when she and her mistress were late in fetching him from his office; if you presume, as I presumed, that he knew she and her cousin were lovers and were keeping him, a trained lawyer of that country which still admits the doctrine of *crime passionelle*, from the only evidence on which a man who kills a faithless wife can be absolutely certain of being acquitted—are there then any gaps, is there any mystery, in the tale?

I think not. Though why he should have told it to me is not quite so evident. Half-confession, surely, cannot be good for even a triple murderer's soul.

FORBIDDEN MUSIC

BY ETHEL MANNIN

FORBIDDEN MUSIC

CHAPTER I

This story within a few thousand words compresses twenty years of a woman's life. To the very young it sounds almost a lifetime; but though twenty years is a long time to look forward to, it is not long in retrospect, and not long in the living. When we are eighteen, thirty-eight sounds completely middle-aged, but even by the time we are twenty-eight we have begun to revise our views on the relativity of age. This, then, is the story of Ishbel Lagan, but it is not her story alone. It is the story of thousands of women. Perhaps it is your story, too.

When Ishbel married John Hedley she was eighteen and he was thirty-two; Ishbel looked, and thought, older than she was; John looked and thought younger, so that the disparity of their years was somewhat modified.

Ishbel, graduating from a commercial

college, went to John's firm as a stenographer; was promoted to being his secretary; flung upon him all unwittingly the golden spell of her youth, reminding him of his own golden years. And she was drawn to him by a quality of simple sincerity which touched responsive chords in herself.

Theirs was a very simple love-story, and they were very happy. They saw the primroses in the Sussex woods at Easter, and the bluebells at Whitsun; they both loved walking, and discovered that they liked the same books and the same things in general. During the summer there were Saturday afternoons and Sundays up the river or in Surrey; the wild roses and the honeysuckle passed, and it was autumn, with a deeper sweetness on the air, something that caught one with an excitement as of spring, yet shook the soul more profoundly. Winter came, with intimate little dinners in Soho restaurants, and, with firelight and drawn curtains and that pervading sense of intimacy, passion, too, took on a deeper note. At the end of the year they were married.

They had a little house at Hampstead, and it seemed as though their happiness must flow on gently like this for ever. Ishbel had no desire to go dancing or to cocktail parties; her life was with her husband in the little house; she was enveloped in the enchantment of love. It did not matter to her that people said that she was "not like a young girl." She merely smiled. She did not feel like a young girl. She felt like a woman. The woman of the man she loved. And she had always been a little grave and more domesticated than was the fashion.

She was nineteen when her child was born. Noel she called her, because she was born at Christmas-time. During the few months before Noel was born began the first of the changes in Ishbel. The fading out of her passion for John was, of course, physio-psychological; there were times when she felt ill and her nerves on edge, and when she worried about the future. There was something so tremendous about motherhood; she was frightened, more than physically, mentally frightened; she did not feel equal to it. There were moments when, curiously, in spite of her love for him, John got on her nerves. He seemed inadequate, sometimes, and his simplicity rather stupid than admirable. And then she would be ashamed of such thoughts and tell herself—and John, too, in fits of contrition—that it was because of her condition, and that when the baby was born she would be her old self.

She could not know, little Ishbel, at nineteen, that there is no going back; that the natural law of evolution is as inexorable as it is inevitable. The changes went on in her relentlessly, unstemmable as the tides, drawn without compunction by the moon. The baby worried her rather. As a little girl she had always loved dolls, and Noel was nothing but a little doll; she worried her, but she could not hand her over to a nurse; she must wash and dress her herself—a little living doll. The thought of any other woman doing things for her baby, child of her body, terrified her, filled her with a curious panic. No, no—little Noel was her baby; no one else could care for her as she could care. Even when her eyes blinded with tears because of Noel's incessant crying, and she, the little-girl mother, not knowing what it was that was the matter. It agonized her when her baby cried, tormented her nerves, too, through the broken nights, but she would not give in and engage a nurse. She couldn't; something in her resisted the idea; her innate, passionate motherhood.

John's nerves were frayed, too; fatherhood was as strange and bewildering for him as motherhood was for Ishbel; more so, for fatherhood is not the violent emotion that motherhood is. He complained bitterly about the broken nights, and he resented the worry that the baby caused Ishbel.

"We ought to have a nurse," he insisted, "we can afford it; you're wearing yourself out; it's ridiculous."

Ishbel read into his complaints an implied criticism of her efficiency as a mother. She resented the implication that a nurse would know better than she did what to do for her baby for the best. John was selfish; he was only thinking of himself; he wanted the baby out of sight and sound—as though he had much to do with her, anyhow! Ishbel's resentment was an appetite that grew with what it fed on. She grew farther and farther away from John, and closer and closer to her baby. She loved him still, sometimes ardently, but she no longer had any illusions about him; she was no longer a young girl blinded by her own ardour. She was a woman who had borne a child, and she saw clearly. She saw him now as a kindly, sincere, entirely ordinary person with a one-track mind and divested of all romantic glamour. He was a dear, of course, but—was this all there was in life? She had a vague idea that she had been cheated.

She had fits of depression which she had never known before her marriage. John said that it was because she was still not strong after having Noel, but she knew in her heart that physically she had never been fitter. She faced the root of her depression in moments of stark honesty. She knew that she was depressed with the realization that here she was at twenty, having run through passion, wifehood and motherhood, and come out on the other side with a sense of spiritual exhaustion. She loved John, but could

o longer deceive herself that she was in
ɔve with him. People said—people who
ad been married a long time, and people
'ho wrote articles for the papers—that
omradeship replaced passion inevitably,
nd compensated for it—but did it, did
;? Wasn't it all self-deception and fox-
nd-the-sour-grapes? At twenty was one
ever to know again the ecstasy of being
apturously in love, living "ready to be
nything in the ecstasy of being ever?"
Vas one to sit down quietly and philo-
ophically at twenty to resignation and
naking the best of things? And could
ne draw warmth from a burnt-out fire?
he told herself passionately that she
'ould not be fobbed off with all this hum-
ug about compensation. She was young,
nd she wanted more of life than second-
ests. Second-best wasn't good enough,
nd it was humbug to pretend it was.
he thought that at twenty—and she was
till thinking it at twenty-five.

But at twenty-five she was less passion-
tely rebellious and more cynically bitter.
Jot bitter against John; poor darling,
'hat could he do about it? He had been
natured when they met; she realized it

now; in spite of his boyishness he woul(never mature any further; she had beer eighteen and only at the beginning of he: evolution as a woman. Were not th• seven years between eighteen and twenty five the most vital in a woman's life– the ones which saw, inevitably, the mos radical mental and emotional changes' No, she was bitter against life; she an(John alike were the victims of it.

She talked a little to some of her un married Neo-Georgian friends. Thes• Bright Young People said at once:

"Good Lord! if you're not happy to gether, why don't you separate?"

As though it was as easy as that. John she knew, was not particularly happy with her—he, too, had been cheated, fo: the woman of twenty-five was not th• girl he had married; ıow could she be —but he would not be happy .part fron her; he was a one-woman man, and sh(was his woman. He had not the tempera ment which seeks consolation elsewhere Neo-Georgians might sneer at his morality as narrow and old-fashioned, but it wa: indomitable and, more, it was funda mental. Ishbel knew that if she left hin

ie would be quite simply—in spite of
ie melodramatic sound the phrase had
-ruining his life, completely shattering
s world. And she, in turn, had not the
mperament that can dance to happiness
ver the ruins of another person's world.
anic would seize her when she would
iink of the utter chaos she had the
ower to impose in another person's life.
Besides, there was Noel. John was
evoted to Noel. He took an immense
ride in her. In those bitter quarrels
hich they had now, which sprang up
ut of the merest trifles, he would declare
assionately that he would never give
oel up. Ishbel could leave him if she
ked, but he would stick to Noel. . . .
nd then a more dreadful and consuming
anic would seize Ishbel. For she, too,
ould not give Noel up—Noel, the child
f her body, her little baby. . . . And
ow her mind would run to and fro, like
rat in a trap, seeking a way of escape
nd finding all the possible exits barred
y her child.

At twenty-eight she began to count the
ears feverishly. Noel was nine; she
ould tell herself, desperately, in another

nine years she would be grown up, capab
of looking after herself; only another ni
years; it wasn't so long, really—hadn
the last nine years passed quickly enough
She had been nineteen, now she wa
twenty-eight; it was nothing; a me
flash in the pan of living—another nir
years would find her only thirty-seve
Once it would have seemed terribly ol
and passé and middle-aged; but now
didn't seem at all middle-aged; wome
kept their youth in these days; at thirt
seven she would still be young—youn
enough to enjoy life, anyhow.

It was in this way that she would com
fort herself, give herself the courage t
go on with that unsatisfactoriness whic
sounds so little on paper, and if one tri
to tell a friend who has not experience
it, but which is so destroying in th
living, so anti-life in the broadest sens
in this way, at twenty-eight, she allie
herself in that lost legion of women-
the valiant, undefeatable defeated!

But before she was thirty she had falle
in love for the second time.

CHAPTER II

ISHBEL had discovered that it tided both her and John over the difficult patches of their life together if occasionally she took a little holiday apart from him. It was for her a sort of sublimation of her constant dream of ultimate escape from this enveloping unsatisfactoriness. She and Noel would go off together for a month, or perhaps longer, and from these little breaks she would gather strength to go on again, keeping the ragged banner flying. Ever since Noel had been five years old they had been going away together for short spells like this, and by the time the child was ten, steamer-berths and *wagons-lits* were for her a part of the natural course of existence.

All her life Ishbel was to remember that it was Noel who suggested that they should go to Italy.

"I'd like to go to Rome," the child announced. Roman legend and history was in her childish imagination. And

Ishbel's imagination in turn fastened upon Italy. Italy! Why not? She was tired of the French Riviera—why not give the Riviera of the Levant a trial, for a change, and work down through Florence to Rome?

They went to Genoa, and from Genoa to Rapallo, and the day after they arrived, sitting and having tea in Aurum's, who should walk in but the Bransons! The Bransons had dropped out of Ishbel's life during the past two years. She did not like them particularly: they made a fetish of doing the fashionable thing—however painful or uncomfortable or inconvenient. The fashionable life, as interpreted by the post-war generation, had never particularly attracted Ishbel, absorbed in her home and child; the "fade out" was mutual; the Bransons and the Hedleys had nothing in common. But here in Rapallo it was different; she was alone and knew no one—and the Bransons liked nothing better than to be able to hail friends at a café—it gave such an air of knowing everybody. They were effusive in their expressions of delight at seeing her, asked her facetiously, with he fashionable cynicism, if she was still iving with her husband, and invited her p to lunch at their villa on the morrow. shbel accepted with genuine gratitude. She even began to feel that she had been ather dull and stodgy not to have liked he Bransons better in the past.

The Bansons' villa was perched romanically on the edge of an olive orchard, nd one climbed to it by way of a steep, narrow, cobbled mule-track up the hillide behind the town.

The Bransons had a guest—Ivor Bansted.

"A genius," said Ronald Branson, with enthusiasm.

"A faun," said Letty Branson, with a smile.

"Both," thought Ishbel, by the end of hat luncheon party.

For Ivor Bansted completely eluded any cataloguing as to type. He was more han good-looking. He had an indefinable Shelleyesque beauty that caused people, both men and women, to turn and look at him a second time, without quite knowing why. Noel fell in love with him at once—and the swift perceptions of children and dogs are significant.

"He's like a fairy person," Noel cried delightedly as she and Ishbel went back down the steep cobbled mule-track.

And it was Noel who suggested the next morning that they should go for a walk back up that mule-track.

"Right past the house where we had lunch," said the child eagerly; "right on as far as ever the path goes."

Ishbel knew that the path went on for miles to the church at the top, and the crest of the hills from whence one may look out over the snow-crowned Apennines. It would be an attractive walk, and she could drop her little conventional note of thanks to the Bransons for the luncheon into their letter-box as she passed. . . .

She let Noel slip the letter into the letter-box. "Don't knock," she told her. She told herself that she did not want the Bransons to think she was passing on the hope of being invited to the house again—but deep down in her something insisted that, more importantly, she did not want Ivor Bansted to know that she was on the hill that morning, lest he should guess how powerfully he had attracted her at that first encounter, how ineradicably he was already in her imagination.

She walked on hurriedly up the steep, difficult path, the olive orchards on either side gleaming like a silver filigree against the deep blue of the sky, glimpses of the warm, glittering blue of the sea meshed like sapphires between their branches. Noel caught her up and they walked on, until a sound of steps behind them caused them instinctively to look back—and they saw Ivor Bansted hurrying towards them, smiling, a tangerine in each hand.

"Isn't his hair gold this morning?" Noel whispered ecstatically.

He came up to them, and Ishbel thought that his eyes were bluer than any sky in Italy.

"I saw you go past the window," he said smiling. "You needn't have hurried so. I've brought some oranges for Noel." He put the tangerines into the child's hands. "I'll walk with you a little way, if I may," he added. "I've nothing to do. Don't the olives look marvellous this morning?"

They walked on until the path turned in another zigzag, and then, at Ivor's suggestion, sat down on a low wall and rested. They talked of Italy. Ishbel mentioned that she was going on to Florence at the end of the week.

"Unless you have to go, that's a mistake," he said. "It will be cold there—and it's so beautiful here. Wait another month before going down to Florence."

"Oh, yes, mummy, let's stay here a long time!" urged Noel, pitching tangerine rind down through the olives as it might be into a blue and silver infinity. "It's so nice here."

But Fate, with blue eyes and a tangerine in each hand, had already settled it. Ishbel lingered in Rapallo, and Ivor joined her and Noel on their mountain walks and picnics, and when the moonlight lay white over the bay and the lighthouse at Portofino—reaching out its dark arm round the bay like a caress—flashed red and green, she and Ivor would go along to Aurum's and drink rum and coffee, and dance, coming out at midnight into the moonlight again, walking through a silver nocturne by the sea-wall. Those golden days, those silver nights, all her life Ishbel remembered. Once again she was living "ready to be anything in the ecstasy of being ever."

One night they did not go to Aurum's, but climbed instead to the gleaming white church that commands the vast ranges of the Apennines. The stars seemed very near up there amongst the mountain peaks, and far, far down below gleamed the shimmering curve of the bay. Ishbel shivered with the sheer ecstasy of so much beauty, and suddenly they were drawn together by the silence and the beauty and that sense of being alone and timeless in infinity. . . . She shivered in his arms in a kind of agony, there in the velvet darkness of the ilex trees, the lonely church unearthly in its whiteness above them, because even in that moment of ecstasy almost too great to bear, reality pressed down upon her—and she remembered little Noel sleeping in the hotel at the foot of the hill—Noel, who barred all ways of escape—Noel who made this agonized ecstasy of love a crime against love.

CHAPTER III

SHE and the child left next day for Florence. She packed feverishly at midnight, and they left by the first train in the morning. From Florence she wrote a brief note to the Bransons begging to be excused for going off without saying good-bye, yet proffering no explanation—for what could she say? To Ivor she did not write at all. She must forget Ivor; get him out of her imagination and out of her blood. She dared not allow herself to love. Life presented her with the choice between a lover and her child—and with all the passionate resistance of her nature she chose her child.

She wandered in Florence, where beauty stands at every street corner, and smiles in its grouped cypresses and encircling hills like an unhappy ghost. Florence was too near to Rapallo—where the sun goes down to a ringing of bells from the wooded hills, and the lighthouse flashes across the glimmering bay; Rapallo where the moonlight leaves the low sea-wall like a silver tide, and the cafés glow behind their trellises. . . .

She went on again, driven by her restlessness, and arrived in Rome; chose for herself a quiet pension abutting on to the Pincio, above the old yellow Spanish steps, and every evening saw the sun go down in a carnival of fire behind St. Peter's—St. Peter's framed in the canopy of ilex trees on the terrace of the Pincio, the ilex trees where dusk gathered early, warm and dark, before the sun had dipped down behind the low hills and the great dome dimmed. . . . Every evening the stately, mournful Roman sunset, and the nuns singing in the old church, and that insistent ache in her heart. . . .

A reproachful letter from the Bransons was forwarded to her from Florence, and she wrote and apologized anew for her abrupt departure and begged them to attribute it to her restlessness, for which, she said, she could not account; but everyone was a little restless these days, weren't they?

A few days later Ivor turned up at the pension. He was hatless and smiling, as on that first morning on the cobbled mule-track.

"I had to come," he said.

All her life Ishbe was to remember, too, those golden mornings on the Palatine, where the wind-flowers blow amid the ruins of pagan temples and imperial palaces, those white Roman nights, with the lights of Frascati gleaming like jewels laid on the velvet darkness across the rolling Campagne. Far and far away now, the little house at Hampstead, and herself in the rôle of Mrs. Hedley. Now she was Ishbel Lagan again, living as she had not lived for ten years in which youth and joy had been drained away; living with every atom of her consciousness, every fibre and nerve of her being—savouring life again as an ecstasy, a vast luxury of living.

Ivor said at last: "You can't go back to Hampstead and being Mrs. Hedley again. It's absurd. Barbarous. Uncivilized. There must be some way out. There's divorce, isn't there?—we'll live in Italy always, you and Noel and I, and all the empty years will seem like a bad dream that's gone by."

And then quite suddenly Ishbel knew that she must go back to England. There was divorce, yes—at a price. And since the price was Noel, she could not buy her freedom. She had heard a pagan music, the pipes of Pan himself, amid the olive-groves of Italy and under the ilex trees, but it was a forbidden music. Not for her to be a happy pagan following in the wake of that soul-drugging music. She must go home.

Ivor was at first impatient, and then angry.

He said: "People aren't as unreasonable as that, Ishbel. No decent man would rob a woman of her child—if your husband ever cared for you at all he couldn't deliberately keep you from happiness now. No; it's simply that you don't love me enough to ask him to divorce you. You are afraid of the insecurity of your life with me—afraid of being poor and afraid of the scandal of a divorce. It means you don't love me, that's all."

She had not thought it possible that any human creature could hurt her so much. Those accusations of Ivor's hurt her so much that all her life, it seemed to her, she carried the scar on her soul. Not love Ivor! Her very soul wept. She could have cried out with the anguish of that injustice.

She came back to England, but not to Hampstead. She took a cottage in the country near Noel's school. She wrote to John at great length, gently, pitifully.

> "You've had the best years of my life" (she wrote), "from eighteen to twenty-eight. Was it my fault that I grew up? How can the woman of twenty-eight be the same person as the girl of eighteen? Another ten years and the last of my youth will be gone—won't you give me those years, for the sake of the years—the best years—that I've given you?"

John wrote also at great length, gently and pitifully—but with a barb, the masculine barb of insistence on "rights," in his reasonableness. Certainly, Ishbel should have her freedom; he did not require any woman to live with him if she did not wish to do so; but there was Noel: one could not have one's cake and eat it;

obviously, of course, he must have the custody of the child.

In anguish Ishbel pleaded with him not to make that condition. It was monstrous that a father should seek to separate a woman from her child: after all she had suffered for that child, a part of her own body. Surely he could not be so cruel? There could be some arrangement by which he could see Noel, and she would promise not to wean the child's affection from him, or to allow her to forget her father.

Piteously she pleaded with him to remember that she herself had been little more than a child when he married her, whereas he had been a mature man of thirty-two. Oh, so often she had heard him refer to his young sister as "only a kid"—but his young sister had been twenty-two—and she, his wife, had been no more than nineteen when she had borne him a child. Hadn't he ever thought of her as "only a kid?" But even as she reminded him of that she knew that he had never thought of her as a child; it might be a crime against youth if his sister had had a child at nineteen—but she was different, because she was his wife and a man had certain "rights" where his wife was concerned.

John Hedley remained adamant. Furthermore, he added that Ishbel had better make up her mind; otherwise he would feel constrained to sue her for restitution of conjugal rights, the which order, if she did not obey, would enable him to divorce her whether she liked it or not; and then, automatically, according to the mechanism of the law in such matters, he would be given the custody of the child.

Ishbel knew when she was defeated. She returned to Hampstead and took up the threads where last she had laid them down. John said, complacently, that he knew she had much too much good sense not to come to her senses sooner or later, and that all this nonsense came of gadding about Italy on her own; in future they would take their holidays together. He had scored over her, and was triumphant in his rôle as the heavy husband. Ishbel—defeated, crushed, raised no resistance.

Only presently, she told herself, presently life itself would release her: another eight years and Noel would be old enough to look after herself; no one could part them then. She must be patient. Another eight years—it wasn't so long, really. Once more she hoisted the ragged banner of the undefeatable defeated.

Ivor wrote from Italy:

"If you loved me enough you would risk it; the law is surely not so barbarous in these enlightened times? Anyhow, some arrangement could be made by which you would not be entirely parted from Noel, could it not?"

She knew then that he did not understand. She would risk her life for him—but not her child. He did not understand—because he was a man, and all laws were man-made—and because men could not love selflessly as women loved, and because he did not comprehend the unthinkable thing he was asking of her. If he loved her as she loved him, he would wait until she could be free without this preposterous price to be paid.

But something in her told her that he would not wait, because she could not make this supreme sacrifice. It would undermine his belief in her love for him. He would shrug his shoulders, man-wise, and allow her to pass out of his life. He would even think of her as a little selfish; unable to make a sacrifice for his sake. "All these motherhood melodramatics!" he would say; for even he, half-genius, half-faun, could be cruel—crueller than any of them, because she loved him.

He came to London in the fulness of time, but they did not meet. He was busy being famous. His first play made an impression on the critics; his second on the public; he was "taken up"; lionized; one read about him in the society gossip of the papers.

CHAPTER IV

NOEL was fifteen when Ishbel heard, indirectly through the Bransons, that he was engaged to be married to the young actress who had played the lead in his latest and most successful play.

Five years had gone by since he kissed her under the ilex trees among the mountain peaks—why should it matter to him any more? It mattered to her now only as a numb ache. She had Noel—a lovely, vivid, brilliant child, and they adored each other, were more like devoted friends than mother and daughter. She had, too, that dream of her freedom that so soon now she would realize. And oh, the blessed, blessed peace of it! A little house of her own, and an end to all this friction and irritation and unsatisfactoriness. She would not want lovers; love was a dream one grew out of, an illusion one learnt not to regret; she was thirty-four now, and all she wanted was a quiet, gracious life, with her friends coming to see her, with her books, her flowers, her simple interests. Oh, she had earned her right to that peace after all these stormy years! She was tired, tired; tired to the bottom of her soul. She and John did not quarrel now, as in their early years. They did not matter enough to each other to quarrel. Hostility had merged into an apathetic indifference. They held together because of Noel—because of Noel's right to have a father as well as a mother; Noel's right to have a home and parents like other children.

They no longer lived in Hampstead. They had a bigger house now, a little way out of London; for now they could afford to run a car and a chauffeur, and John was no longer dependent on train services. They had a big garden that was a delight to Ishbel and one of the compensations of her home-life. The landscape gardeners—who laid out the garden—found her a stone figure of Pan, which she placed near the garden seat because she liked to sit there and dream of Italy and a sweet, forbidden music that played among the olive-groves. Behind this figure of Pan was a slender young poplar which at dusk reminded her of sentinel cypresses on the hillsides of Rapallo, and in sunlight of the silver filigree of the olives poised between the Della Robbia blue of sea and sky. All the hurt of that Italian idyll had passed now, and she remembered only its beauty.

Noel was sixteen, seventeen. Nearer and nearer drew the dream of freedom now. Ah, then she would be revenged on John for all this waste of life, for the loss of Ivor, for the empty, wasted years! All her youth he owed her, and her right to love. The best of her life he had had, the passionate spring and the glowing summer; but there was a sweetness in the fall of the year, and he should not rob her of that too. When Noel was eighteen she would tell her. Even if John insisted that his daughter went on living with him it would not matter; he would not be able to keep her away from her mother if she chose to come and visit her —as, of course, she would. For Noel at eighteen would understand. She would understand all the sacrifices her mother had made for love of her; would love her all the more because of them.

There was a party on Noel's eighteenth birthday—all Noel's friends from London University, where, modernly, she was studying science along with her male contemporaries. Very lovely looked Noel on her eighteenth birthday, with her shining hair, and her gossamer dress like the wings of a yellow butterfly. And when the last guest had gone, and John, who hated sitting up late, had gone to bed, Noel and her mother sat on the veranda overlooking the garden and smoked and talked, and Ishbel worked round to the subject which had been her dream for nearly as many years as Noel had walked the earth.

"Dear," she said, taking the girl's hands, "I've waited for this night so long. Waited for you to grow up—I've been so unhappy all these years. I was married when I was your age, Noel."

"Nothing like that about this generation," the girl replied. "But I guess yours and dad's generation had more staying-power."

"It's not always the question of staying-power, darling; sometimes it's a question of—the custody of the child. Don't you understand, Noel? I waited for you to grow up—and to-night you're grown up."

The girl turned startled eyes to her. "What do you mean? You're not telling me that you'd have left dad but for me?"

Ishbel nodded. "Yes; and now that you're not a little girl any longer—I'm free. Oh, Noel, you don't know what a relief it is to be able to tell you at last." She wanted to feel her daughter's arms round her, but instead Noel jumped to her feet, stood leaning against the veranda rail, staring at her incredulously.

"But this is dreadful, mother! At your age—after all these years—wanting to leave dad! He's an angel—and he adores you!"

Ishbel laughed bitterly. "Parents must keep up appearances before their children, Noel. He hasn't been any happier than I have—not quite so actively unhappy, perhaps, but not happy."

"And you're proposing to make him less happy! It's a shame! It's ghastly!

You must be crazy, mother. What will everyone say? It's not as if you were a young couple. It's ridiculous and—and—beastly——"

And quite suddenly the yellow butterfly had flung away from the veranda and rushed away through the starlight of the garden.

CHAPTER V

Ishbel sat quite still, not daring to formulate her thoughts. It was as though she sat motionless lest moving realization should bear down upon her. It was John who disturbed her. He had come downstairs in his dressing-gown. His voice when he spoke was petulant.

"I saw Noel go down the garden some time ago when I was undressing," he said, "and she hasn't come back yet. What is she doing? She'll get a chill outdoors at this time of the night without anything round her in that thin dress. It's time she was in bed, anyway."

Ishbel rose.

"Yes; she said she wanted some air. I'll go and find her." She hesitated a moment, then turned to John. "It all went off very well—the party, I mean," she said awkwardly.

The petulance drained from his face and he smiled.

"Yes, yes, splendidly. Noel eighteen—

think of it!" There was paternal pride in his voice.

"I was eighteen when we first met," Ishbel said in a low voice.

"Yes." He was silent a moment, as though he pondered the thought, then suddenly he stepped close to her. "It's a sort of anniversary for us, too," he said, and took her hands. He went on, almost pleadingly: "It—it hasn't been such a bad nineteen years, has it? Difficult, of course, but marriage always is, I suppose—and——" he laughed self-consciously—"we've survived it."

"Yes. We've survived it." She gave his hand a little squeeze as a gust of emotion swept her. She said hurriedly: "I'll go and find the child and remind her about bed."

"Right-o!" He turned away and went back into the room humming under his breath. He was content, easily reassured. He did not ask ecstasy of life. Well, neither did she any more. He cared about their daughter—fussed over her getting a cold in the night air; whilst she, her mother, immersed in her own emotions, had forgotten. It was as though life had crept up to her and nudged her reproachfully.

She drew her beaded shawl about her over her bare shoulders and stepped off the veranda on to the lawn.

She found Noel sitting on the garden seat, her arms flung out over the pedestal of the statue of Pan, her head on her arms. She was crying. Pan smiled down at her, his satyr's sardonic smile.

Ishbel put her arms round the girl.

"Dear," she whispered huskily, "it's all right. Your father and I love each other—it's only that sometimes we both get a little tired—marriage isn't easy, dear. You mustn't mind what people say when they're tired."

She was aware of two arms flung round her, white in the dim starlight.

"Mummy, darling, I knew you couldn't mean it! I love you both so much! You're both such darlings—I couldn't bear you to leave dad. We've been such pals always, daddy and I!"

"Yes, yes, darling; it's all right; run in now; it's cold and you must be tired. I'm just going to sit here and have another cigarette before I turn in."

Noel kissed her again and ran over the lawn. Ishbel sat there, but she did not smoke. She looked up at Pan in the starlight, and presently she, too, bowed her head at his feet. Not for her the sweet forbidden music; he played for gods, and she was mortal clay, drawn earthwards by mortal hands, warm hands that clung so that one could follow only in dreams the goat-foot god. . . . Noel's love for her father—she had reckoned without that. . . . No wonder Pan of the sweet forbidden music wore that sardonic smile.

Now John was coming across the lawn in his dressing-gown, a little grotesque under the stars.

"Bless my soul," he said, exasperation in his voice, "the craze you women have got for sitting about in the damp night air! You'll catch your death."

She rose, laughing a little unsteadily.

"It's so hot in the house after the party," she said, and suddenly caught at his hands.

"John, do you ever think of me when I was eighteen when you look at Noel?"

"Always. Why do you ask?" His voice was suddenly sombre.

"Because—oh, John, because I want you to!"

He put his arm round her and kissed her.

"I thought you looked wonderfully young to-night, Ishbel," he said in a low, curiously shaken voice. "I—I kind of wished we hadn't grown so—so far apart, as it were. Kind of wished we might step back over the years."

"We can," she whispered, sudden tears in her voice, "we can."

They walked back to the house together, their arms about each other, like lovers. Pan smiled in the gentle darkness, perhaps a little wistfully.

Produced in conjunction with
The Readers Library Publishing Co., Ltd.